PRAISE FOR CATHERINE FEARNS

A fascinating historical drama... a deep look into the fear of witchcraft underscoring how gender and sex were at the heart of it.

— KIRKUS REVIEWS

All the Parts of the Soul combines meticulous historical research with a twisting, pulsating plot that reveals the horrors and hypocrisy of the Geneva witch trials in a brutal yet brilliant fashion. Catherine Fearnes pulls no punches and delivers a dark, disturbing work of literary fiction that will live long in the minds of those who read it.

— STEPHEN BLACK, AUTHOR OF *THE KIRKWOOD CHRONICLES*

ALL THE PARTS OF THE SOUL

CATHERINE FEARNS

ALL THE PARTS OF THE SOUL
By CATHERINE FEARNS
Published by QUILL & CROW PUBLISHING HOUSE

Cover Design by Fay Lane

Interior by Cassandra L. Thompson

Printed in the United States of America

ISBN (ebook) 978-1-958228-26-5

ISBN (print) 978-1-958228-27-2

Library of Congress Control Number: 2023911087

Publisher's Website: www.quillandcrowpublishinghouse.com

"All the fierce animals you see are armed for your destruction. But if you try to shut yourself up in a walled garden, seemingly delightful, sometimes a serpent lies there hidden."

— JOHN CALVIN, INSTITUTES

"For the penalty of death is not inflicted except for some grave and notorious crime, but it is otherwise with death of the soul, which can be brought about by the power of a phantastical illusion or even by the stress of temptation."

— MALLEUS MALEFICARUM

PUBLISHER'S NOTE

It is important that history be told without censorship. Since this novel is based on actual historical documentation, please be advised that some of the material may be sensitive in nature. For a full list of potentially triggering content, please see Appendix B. For translations and explanation of the Latin chapter names, please see Appendix A.

PREFACE

CATHERINE FEARNS

From fairytales and folklore to Disney and Halloween, we are all enchanted by the idea of a witch, and witchcraft imagery is ubiquitous in our culture and consciousness. But the witches in this book are not romantic, ethereal, gothic, and mysterious. Nor are they wicked old hags. They are ordinary women.

The true story of the European witch craze is a tragedy of unimaginable cruelty and violence. Between the 15th and 17th century, tens of thousands of innocent people were tortured and killed, the majority of them women. Usually their only crime was to be different.

This book tells the story of a small group of those women, in the Calvinist city of Geneva in 1545. It is not for the faint-hearted. When I was researching this book, I was continually shocked by what occurred, but it is my firm belief that truth in all its horrors should be confronted.

So be prepared for uncomfortable reading. Witch-hunting still means something today, and there is a potential witch-hunter in all of us when we hold up a mirror to our souls.

History is made by historians, and in recent years there has been a welcome revolution in women's history, with women's roles being written back in. From my children's textbooks, I am learning about figures who went unmentioned when I was a history student.

But the history of women is also the history of misogyny. So as well as giving voice to those whom history has silenced, we must also examine the voices of those who did the silencing – so we can hold them accountable and understand their motives. It is for this reason that I chose the perspective I did.

In a world where violence against women continues at epidemic levels, and religious hypocrisy still justifies all manner of intolerances, we do history no favours by glossing over the darkest parts of the soul.

- Catherine Fearns, Geneva, 2023

CRIMEN EXCEPTUM

SEPTEMBER 4, 1545

When I was a boy of twelve, I saw a long-tailed star. It was a hot night, and stagnant air hung heavy over the city under plague curfew. Rue Tabazan was deserted save for the crier, who paced slowly, ringing the warning bell. In my childish zeal to contribute to civic duty like my father, I leaned over the window frame, watching for curfew-breakers or, more thrilling, the plague-spreaders. Sometimes I would sit for hours, not knowing what I would do if I actually saw one of those servants of the Devil.

But on that particular night, I was distracted from my vigil by a white light in the sky. Far across the lake, it lit the snowy peaks of the Mont Blanc so I could discern every ridge and contour, like a secret glimpse of Heaven itself. In awe, I shook my elder brother awake.

He was unwilling at first, but when I finally persuaded him to stagger half-asleep to the window, his eyes also widened in amazement.

"What is it, Pierre?" I asked, unable to look away. "Is it an angel?"

"It is a portent of some sort; that's for certain."

We watched the star continue its passage, slow and steady across the sky, with a tail that quivered like white fire. And we prayed for good fortune, for how could anything so beautiful forewarn of ill?

Within a month, Pierre was dead—my mother, father, and baby

sister too. The baby went first, and my mother might have died of a broken heart had she not been afflicted herself. My brother held out the longest. I sat with him at the Plague Hospital and watched him suffer in blood and pus and feces until it pleased God to take him too, and then I was alone in the world.

It was the greasers. There is no doubt; they had been active in our part of town, and my father, as a merchant and councilman, certainly had no shortage of enemies. Greasers, plague-spreaders, *bouteurs de peste, engraisseurs*—call them what you will. Call them demons—for the very idea could only come from Hell itself. These evil conspirators hack the rotting limbs from plague victims to concoct an unguent or powder to smear on door handles. For an ephemeral chance at profit, to raid the houses of the dead. Or worse, out of enmity or jealousy—petty neighborhood squabbles becoming unimaginable evil and torture.

Had I not been distracted by that star, perhaps I would have seen them and been able to prevent what happened.

At least this particular conspirator was caught and punished. I watched a woman burn for it in the Field of Execution at Champel. I knew the Devil was there for when I saw her shaved head and sex, and the weals and bruises on her broken body, I felt the first ever stirrings in my loins. As the flames licked around her and she screamed in pain and terror, I felt *la petite mort* for the first time. I knew then the dangers of the lustfulness of women. Even at the moment of her death, she tempted me. It would be my lot in life to be tempted and to resist. I also saw the power of the magistracy that could right these wrongs, in Geneva at least, and knew that I would devote my life to bringing about God's justice on Earth.

My brother had been right about the portent—in the fifteen years since, it has pleased God to trial Geneva with such misery and suffering that it has often seemed like the Tribulation itself is upon us. With the papacy revealed as the seat of the Antichrist, Calvin and the city fathers are building the new Rome here in Geneva; thus, the new faith and its people are under attack from the forces of Hell.

The plague is upon us again, worse than ever. I sometimes wonder if I am immune, having survived so many bouts in such close proximity to sufferers, but I take all the precautions nevertheless. I have perfected the art of never touching a door handle. I never leave the house without scented pomanders, my only extravagance in life. I wear them around my neck and attached to my belt, and I hold a vinegar-soaked cloth to my mouth while weaving through the streets—so crowded are we within these city walls that I could not avoid the dreaded miasma otherwise. Indeed, my whole life since my parents died has been devoted to avoiding people, and I have succeeded as well as can be expected in a city so teeming.

Today, I stepped even more gingerly than usual across the cobblestones, determined to keep my robes and shoes clean. I had been summoned by the great John Calvin himself. Our city's savior and mentor stays close to his people, with all welcome at his twice-weekly St. Peter's Cathedral sermons, from the grandest prince to the poorest beggar. Indeed, Calvin himself is a refugee from the heresy of his native France. Still, to be personally invited to his home was an honor I did not expect so early in my career.

Calvin lives in a fine, though relatively modest, house on the rue de Chanoines, gifted to him by the council as part of the negotiations for his return from exile. I hesitated before touching the iron knocker, then reproached myself, for surely only the Devil himself would dare grease the door of John Calvin.

It was opened by his wife, Idelette de Bure—no housekeeper or fanfare and, although she wore fashionable wide sleeves and expensive lacework on her collar and cap, she was dressed modestly, one might even say severely, in black. She ushered me through with a sort of weary friendliness, as if she is used to a constant stream of visitors. "You are in luck, Monsieur Aubert. His last meeting ended earlier than expected, so you can go straight into his chamber."

Before I knew it, the door opened and I was thrust into the library of the great Calvin himself. Scrolls and leather-bound books lined the shelves from floor to ceiling, with more piled on the floor and open on his desk. Although I am an avid collector of books, I had never seen so many in one place.

He was almost buried in them, which may have added to the surprising impression that he is physically fragile. He must have been around forty years old, but he looked older, his wide eyes sunken, cheekbones prominent, with a graying beard almost absurdly long, dwindling to a point over his chest where it blended with the fur of his robe. He wore a close-fitting black cap and plain black robes, a rich fur throw his only concession to luxury. So engrossed was he in the letter he wrote, that Idelette had to introduce me twice before he looked up. Even then, he did not put his quill down. "Husband, here is Henry Aubert, city magistrate, as you requested."

"Ah, Aubert, please sit." He motioned to the chair across from him, and I sat and waited while he wrote. Finally, he signed the paper, put his quill down, and spoke as he sealed the letter. "My apologies. I can barely keep up with all this correspondence. Our brothers in Strasbourg." He nodded to the letter. "Wrestling heresy with the full armor of God." He smiled as he put it aside to give me his full attention. "Now, why have I asked you here today? I see you are the youngest magistrate on the council, Monsieur Aubert. Very impressive. How did you manage it?"

I bowed my head. "I am twenty-nine years old, sir. I have been a notary since my apprenticeship, and it was my honor to be selected for the magistracy in the February elections."

How strange it was to hear my own voice, speaking phrases unplanned, responding to a conversation as if it were nothing. It was uncharted territory. My work as a notary provides very little human interaction; I go to the town hall, listen, write, and return to my empty house.

"Legal training and of modest background. Very much like myself." He smiled with such warmth that I filled with pride.

"My father was a shoemaker."

"Head of the shoemakers' guild, no less. And a councilman himself. You lost your family at a young age; I am sorry for you. I too lost my mother very young. These trials can never truly be overcome—although, with God's grace, we persevere. You were taught by Froment and lived with him too, I believe?"

"Yes, I went to his classes at Molard every day in the months after my parents died. He and his wife were very kind; they saw my potential and sponsored me to go to the College Rive and obtain my training and apprenticeship. I will be forever indebted to them."

When I was alone in those months after my family died, only daring to leave the house when I was so hungry, I could no longer bear it, I saw Antoine Froment in the Place du Molard, announcing his classes and putting up notices. He offered free schooling to any who wished, claiming he could teach anyone to read and write within three months.

Every day, I went to the Grande Salle du Boitet, at the sign of the Croix d'Or, with the other children of Geneva. I already knew how to read and write, but Froment also taught us the true Christian religion. These were revolutionary days and, while soldiers and men of politics fought for our freedom from foreign princes, children and preachers were on the frontline of our spiritual battle for the reformed faith. Most children went home to pass it on to their parents, and I envied them. I had no one to teach. But Froment and his wife, Marie Dentière, saw something in my abilities and encouraged me to take up an apprentice-ship. I kept much from them, and they knew nothing of my true situa-tion. Certainly, I will not tell Calvin how I really lived during my teenage years, alone in an empty house. But still, they saved my life, and I vowed to devote it to civic duty and the building of a truly godly city, as they did.

Calvin looked at me kindly. "You have honored your family's memory."

I was stunned he knew so much about me and made some bland attempt at a reply. "It has pleased God to trial our city with such a manner of horrors. I fear this latest bout of plague is the worst yet."

"And that is exactly why you are here, my son. There is a situation, and I would like you to assist. Have you been to Satigny?"

I had not, and had no wish to, for everyone knew of its infamy. Satigny is a *mandement*, an administrative district, of Geneva but some-thing of an outlier, particularly since the city walls went up. A half day's ride from the cathedral, it is a rural area, a scattering of villages in the shadow of the Jura and on the border with Savoy. A strategic outpost, perhaps, but its inhabitants' main contribution to the city this year, other than wine, has been a notorious bout of plague-spreading. Back in the spring, no less than forty people burned for it. The year's plague still rages in the city and brings back painful memories.

"I confess I have not."

"No matter. In any case—the place is overrun."

"Surely not the Savoyards?"

"No, no. Although you are correct that, with the whole *mandement* surrounded by Savoy, loyalties to Geneva have not been fully established. No, no, I'm talking about witches. The whole place appears to be crawling with witches."

"Witches? I only know about the plague-spreaders captured there."

"Plague-spreaders, witches, what is the difference? They are one and the same. It is all the work of the Devil. The council received a supplication from Donzel, the *châtelain* of Satigny. A prominent farmer's wife has accused her lying-in maid of witchcraft, and now accusations fly. I want you to go out there and assist."

I must have looked stunned, so he continued.

"With the local population decimated by war and plague—the bailiff died in the spring so there's only Donzel left with any authority—they have neither the prisons, the legal expertise, nor the equipment to deal with this situation. They are so understaffed they can't cope with another set of trials. And they made a terrible mess of the last ones, which should have been transferred to the city. There is still a lot of unruliness there. You have assisted at criminal trials before, have you not?"

My head spun. "Yes, theft, usury, and other financial cases. But are these not matters for church courts?"

"No, no, the Church is far too busy with heretics. These are, and must be, civil matters. Indeed, heresy is now a civil matter, since church and state are now one in Geneva. You have witnessed witch trials already, have you not?"

I felt myself grow hard again as I recalled my last witch burning. I redden to think of the effect it had on me, the tingle in my loins while I watched the young woman burn. But surely, we all feel this way. "Yes. But, upon my honor, I do not feel worthy of—"

"Monsieur Aubert, these are momentous times. Perhaps the End Times or, with God's grace, just the beginning. Either way, we must all do our part. Peace is fragile, and we must bring the rural districts into line, or the Savoyards will be back in no time. And as for Berne... We are their veritable slaves and that displeases me. The rural communities do not have the same morals as the city people I have educated. We are building a new moral realm here in Geneva, and that must extend to the villages as well. Furthermore, as the Senate continues to remind me, we need Satigny. Much as I would like to keep us all in our fortress behind these city walls, the coffers are almost empty—the wine cellars are almost empty. There is wealth to be tapped in Satigny. You will see how glorious their fields and vine-yards are."

I opened my mouth to speak, simply because I had been listening for a long time and perhaps it was my turn.

He stopped and gestured for me to continue, but I had nothing and only succeeded in interrupting.

I curse myself for my ineptitude in all these situations.

But he seemed to understand and, to my relief, continued. "This is a glorious opportunity to strike against heresy, and a glorious opportunity for your own advancement. Use the full force of the law to secure some convictions for us, Monsieur Aubert, convictions that shall be well-promoted abroad. You will be amply rewarded for your efforts."

Having gotten over the initial jolt to my senses, I decide that I should be thrilled with the opportunity. To see my hard work and abilities rewarded—it would truly be a new world. I bow solemnly. "It is my honor to serve the city. To help you build a new society. When shall I begin? How shall I begin?"

"Immediately, my friend. Wrap up your affairs here and set out on the morrow. It is only a three hours' ride. If all goes well, you will not have to stay long; indeed, it is far better if the accused can be tried here in the city where everyone can see them. Although, on the other hand, you would do well to be out of the city at this time. It is September; by the time this is over, winter will almost be upon us, and the cold always seems to kill off the plague, does it not?" With that, he appeared to go back to his work, taking up a document and quill.

But still, I hovered. He was entrusting me with life and death and had given me almost no instruction.

As if sensing my insecurity, he looked up again. "Do you have a copy of the *Malleus?*"

"The *Malleus?*"

"*Malleus Maleficarum.* The Hammer of Witches. It was written more than half a century ago now, but it has become something of a manual. Highly respected work. I believe it is the most published book in the whole of Europe, after the Bible. What does that tell us, eh? Here, I will lend you mine. You can use it as a guide for conducting your investigation. It's still only in Latin at the moment. In fact, I must commission a French edition."

He handed me a heavy leather-bound volume, and I clutched it to my chest, still hovering.

In truth, I felt the ground moving beneath my feet. If I could just have had some time to think about it all. "If I may, Monsieur Calvin, why did you choose me? I am the most junior of all the magistrates you could have selected. I have no experience in these matters at all."

"Witchcraft is a *crimen exceptum.* You don't need experience—you need initiative." He could tell I was not convinced, so he put his quill down and came around the desk to put a hand on my shoulder. "I know you have been cruelly touched by the horror of plague-spreading, so you have an even greater incentive than most to..."

I waited for him to say 'avenge,' but he considered his choice of words. "To want justice done."

"But plague-spreading is conspiratorial poisoning—it's not the same as witchcraft, surely."

"Does it matter?" he dismissed. "Both are the work of Satan. Both present an opportunity to lead people back to God. And also..." He pauses and smiles in an almost fatherly manner. "I want someone I can mold into my successor. You are young and talented. As I said, witchcraft is a *crimen exceptum*—normal rules don't apply, and...creativity, shall we say, is not only permitted, but advised. It is even an advantage to have a novice magistrate or one not trained in the law. We must beat the Devil at his own game."

"Regarding that, Monsieur Calvin, what about persuasive techniques? It is my understanding that witchcraft confessions are almost never obtained without torture."

"Ah yes. Well, you may use whatever means are at your disposal in Satigny. I don't know what it is they do over there. You have the *Malleus* to guide you. When it comes to the strappado and the barber-surgeons, by that point, you should have transferred proceedings to the city for the trial. And I have no doubt there will be a trial. Or even trials... You know how these things escalate."

"And if I find the accused to be innocent?"

I could not read his expression then, though I felt I was supposed to.

"You will find what you find," he said. "But you are tasked to investigate. Any trial should take place here, in public view."

And, with that strange mixture of pragmatism and dogmatism, fervor and calm, he showed me towards the door, and then took me in his arms. It appeared the meeting was over. Although I was almost a head taller than him, especially with his stoop, I felt my face buried in the musty depths of his fur collar. I tensed and shrank at first, then I relaxed into his grip, feeling oddly tearful. I realized it was the first time I had been touched in a very long time, perhaps since I was a child, and as his body pressed against mine, I tried with all my might to shut out visions of witches being tortured. A power now entrusted to me.

He released me from his grip but continued to hold my upper arms, looking up at my face. "How handsome you are! And not married yet? You must marry, my boy! It is the only honorable state for a Christian man."

I had no reply, so he continued.

"I suppose without parents to find you a suitable match... I will help, don't worry." He winked, and I was mortified.

INDEX LIBRIUM PROHIBITUM

SEPTEMBER 5, 1545

Sleep has never come easily to me, and I usually stay up into the early hours of the morning, reading, writing, and watching from the window. These are the loneliest hours, but I am not lonely —I am with my thoughts, my diary and, most of all, my books. I own quite a collection. Geneva has several printing presses, and I am a regular visitor to the book stalls in the Place du Molard, which receives interesting new works from the Frankfurt Book Fair and passing tradesmen.

Of course, with Calvin being keen to purge the city of unclean acts and unclean thoughts, the Index of Prohibited Books is extensive in Geneva. More books are being banned by the consistory every week, so most of what I can obtain is religious and philosophic.

It is odd, though, that so many of these texts seem to intensify the very desires they command us to suppress. The Penitentials castigate a variety of carnal sins in great detail. One of the volumes I read most is the Bishop of Worms's *Decretum*; I can still hardly believe the depths of depravity to which women apparently stoop. Fashioning large implements and devices to place within themselves for pleasure or, worse, attaching these implements to their genital areas in a mockery of masculinity? Placing a live fish within themselves and leaving it there until it is dead, then roasting and feeding it to their husbands to make their love more ardent? This is obscene sorcery committed by common housewives. One cannot imagine what a real witch would do. Or perhaps all women are witches at heart.

I often find shocking images scribbled in the margins of second-hand liturgical manuscripts: beasts with giant members, women with splayed legs, fantastical multi-limbed creatures copulating in bizarre fashions. Perhaps the priests who drew the images wished to remind us that temptation is everywhere—and that we must resist it. So, when I lock myself away to wrestle with temptation, strangely, I do see it as a spiritual act.

I have plenty of secular materials too, as I am fortunate enough to have had a book-loving father. He worked himself from poverty to the shoemaking business, grew wealthy enough to purchase Genevan citizenship and a place on the Small Council, and, although he did not read well, viewed books as a symbol of his elevated status.

I inherited the works of Catallus and the *Priapeia*—poems so scandalous it is no wonder the city banned them. I have seen two book-sellers imprisoned for attempting to sell copies of Catallus, but I see no reason to surrender mine, as it would only draw attention to me. My father even owned a strange Catalan book—well-hidden when he was alive—entitled *A Mirror for Fuckers*, which details innumerable and impossible entanglements between men and women, even between men and men, women and women. When I read and reread these sorts of books, it is only so I can better understand the minds of the depraved. Because surely these things are impossible outside the imagination.

When I tire of reading, I write in my journals. How easy it is to express myself by means of the written word. Would that we never had to open our mouths! Although Froment taught me to write in French, and it is the language encouraged in all things now, I prefer to write my diaries in Latin. There is something liberating about being so detached from what I am communicating. Even though, in truth, I am only communicating with myself.

But my most important occupation when I am at home is to watch out of the window—especially when the plague is raging. This is the place where I saw the fiery star. This is where I was distracted that night, when the plague-spreaders must have basted the door with the unguent that killed my family. This is the position I must take, ever watchful. Had I only been more watchful that night, perhaps things would be very different. So, this is my penance, my atonement, my torture, my pleasure. Because there is much to see in our busy streets, and it is not so terrible to watch the world go by. When it is quiet at night, I have my imaginings to keep me company. An unknown guardian of the city, I anchor myself here, a constant amidst the constantly changing, a silent watchman. And it brings me comfort.

I knew last night would be no exception to my insomnia, so anxious am I about the adventure ahead. And, in any case, I had a new book to read—the *Malleus Maleficarum*. By candlelight, I devoured it, turning the pages with the measured thrill of one who has perhaps found the book he has been searching for his whole life. It was written in the Rhineland, late last century, by Jacob Sprenger, an inquisitor and also a Dominican friar—so, by all accounts, a godly man. It was granted a Papal bull and, while we no longer recognize the Pope, that stamp of authority confirms its status as a reliable text.

The *Malleus* explains so many of the world's ills. Since Eve first took a bite of the apple, women are to blame for so much. Indeed, the book says, "If we inquire, we find that nearly all the kingdoms of the world have been overthrown by women." This is a true work of scholarship, corroborated throughout by evidence from the scriptures as well as confessions from witches. The first part of the book provides a definitive justification for the reality of sorcery and the need to extirpate it. The citations from scripture are too innumerable to even mention. Suffice to quote Exodus: "Thou shalt not permit a sorceress to live." Put simply, if the Devil exists—and it would be heresy to deny it—then witchcraft must also exist. Because witches cannot perform their evil tasks without the help of the devil, with whom they must enter a pact.

The *Malleus* also justifies my role in the process and gives me confidence that it is my sacred duty, since women are so weak, to protect the world of men from their wiles and the wiles of the Devil. It explains what Calvin insinuated: that sorcery has the criminal status of heresy—which is logical, since a witch must go against God—and that secular courts can and should use inquisitorial practices to extirpate witches. Of course—why had I not realized it before? This is my justification, and now I feel better. Despite my relative inexperience, I am qualified for these investigations after all.

The second part of the book deals with the activities of sorceresses themselves, and how to prevent them. The details are shocking. The accused must engage in six different activities to qualify as a sorceress. These consist of a pact with the Devil, sexual relations with the Devil, aerial flight, assembly at a sabbath, magic, and the slaughter of babies. A witch is occasionally a man, but usually a woman, and Sprenger did extensive and impressive research to explain why it is women that are the weaker and more terrifying sex. They are far less constant in their faith and therefore far more likely to be swayed by the Devil. They are also insatiable in their sexual desire, which cannot be sated by mortal man. Concubines are the most wicked, followed by midwives, then women who dominate their husbands. These facts were shocking enough to read, but the *Malleus* goes into surprising detail, such is the diabolical filthiness that must be addressed.

There were parts of the book that made me blush, that made me sweat. The temptations to which men are exposed, the filthiness and debauchery of women. It is hard to believe some of the things mentioned. Things I would love and hate to see with my own eyes, that might scar me forever, things that could only have been invented in Hell.

A woman writhing in pleasure with an invisible demon? Kissing the Devil's backside, licking his anus? His enormous, spiked member and ice-cold semen? I can hardly bear to write the words. Rendering an innocent man impotent or, worse, stealing his member? The grinding down of babies' bones to make a powder, the roasting of a baby's organs, and the drinking of its blood—such gruesome activities almost pale in comparison to the depths of sexual depravity to which women are capable. How can such things be written? Who could even think of such things? And yet I was struck by a strange sense of familiarity as if these visions had already been there, just waiting to be developed. And since no one could simply imagine something so depraved, perhaps it must come from real life.

I felt guilty even for reading the book, shocked and delighted in equal measure that Calvin himself gave it to me. Had his eyes really taken in these very words? These images must be in his mind too. I am terrifyingly and deliciously out of my depth, swimming in filth, yet authorized to do so.

The final part of the book is most certainly a manual. It provides a step-by-step guide to conducting a witch investigation and trial, from the questions I should ask at each stage, to the requirements for witnesses, defense...and torture. The tools at my disposal are extensive, for the *Malleus* recommends deception as well as torture. I may deceive the accused as much as necessary and make promises I am not obliged to keep. For we must use all the tools at our disposal in this battle against the Devil. The aim is to secure a conviction, and our faith can be placed in God's justice, for God would never permit an innocent to be convicted of witchcraft. So, we can be sure of ourselves in the knowledge that whatever we do must be God's will. I am not quite ready to imagine myself conducting torture, but it is a notion that ignites my bones, and I will save my thoughts on that for another time. A gift to myself.

Any skepticism I may have had is gone. Calvin is right, and all this must be brought into the open and extirpated so we can form our godly society. Whether or not this is, as he says, the beginning of the end of times.

When I finally fell into a fitful sleep, I tossed and turned and dreamt of the obscene kiss, over and over. And it is not a sin to be tempted, for even St. Jerome and St. Antony were tempted in the desert as a test of their faith. I am constantly testing my faith in this way; indeed, it is my duty as a man of God. When my loins swell, I revel in the battle against the onanism which Calvin tells us Genevans is such a monstrous sin. He is not the first—Luther tells us that the secret sin, the pollution of one's own flesh is worse than rape, since rape at least is within the natural order of things. And, on Thomas Aquinas's hierarchy of perversions (a list to which I frequently and in detail refer), the unchaste softness, as he calls it, ranks above bestiality and sodomy.

But when the moment sometimes comes, I do not worry—for it is against my will. It is the work of the Devil, from whom our souls are under constant attack. And since Calvin does say it is the "involuntary spilling of semen" that is the sin, and I do believe he is referring more to the practice of *coitus interruptus* than to the private moment itself, I am not overly concerned.

SINE DIABLO, NULLUS DOMINUS

SEPTEMBER 6, 1545

Early this morning, I locked up the house, not knowing whether I would return in one day or many and not caring since that house has only ever been filled with sadness. There was no one to whom I needed to say goodbye since I had never employed so much as a housekeeper. Alone since the age of twelve, I am capable and self-reliant; I have need for no one, and, furthermore, I desire no one.

I have perfected a method of slamming the door without touching that infernal handle, and the long iron key I keep on a rope around my neck allows me to lock it from a safe distance. The handle is in the shape of a demon, the knocker in its mouth causing it to grin devilishly, a cruel taunt every time I enter or leave. Instead of warding evil from my family home, the demon invited her in. You may wonder why I did not have it removed or changed to something more innocuous. Apart from the fact that nobody, least of all me, wants to touch it and so taint themselves with its curse, I get a perverse pleasure from the reminder that the Devil is everywhere—a reminder to keep myself alone and protected.

I tossed a coin to the two boys carrying my saddle bag containing spare undergarments, my precious diary, and my copy of the *Malleus*.

This left my hands free to buy provisions for the journey as we wove through the market stalls just opening for the day.

Since the walls went up in 1536 and the suburbs were brought in, we are falling over each other in this tiny city. We live on top of each other, literally, as new stories are added to houses already teetering. The end of curfew bell had only rung an hour before, and the streets were already so crowded that tipcarts, pails, and baskets constantly blocked my path, and my senses were overloaded with mingled stenches. I could barely keep up with the boys as they expertly darted from side to side, their bare feet dodging horse manure and my bag knocking apples from the carts of furious merchants. I opened my umbrella, knowing it was a prime time of day for the emptying of chamber pots from upstairs windows.

We arrived at the city livery, and I collected a fine chestnut mare, loaned to me by the council, that I could hardly believe was mine for the duration of the case. I am not an expert rider, but after several clumsy attempts at mounting, the mare yielded, and we sauntered down to the lakeside, where she took a drink before the journey. I looked out across the water. In the morning haze, there was barely any difference between the lake, the mountains, and the sky—it looked as if the Earth had risen to meet Heaven itself. The Alps and the Valais were invisible, yet I knew they were there, like a reminder of the presence of God. Only a fishing boat coming in silently with a morning catch revealed it to be water at all. The expanse of pale blue filled my soul with promise and the spirit of our new city, which would triumph.

But that was to be my last glimpse of the lake for a while, I knew because I was turning towards the Jura, towards my assigned and ominous task. Where the lake view and the Alps had been all pale blues and whites, the Jura range was dark green with looming gray clouds. When I reached the city gates, two hanging bandits swung gently from their gallows high above my head, the last of the summer's bluebottles buzzing around them. A reminder to all of the penalties of deviance, and a reminder to me of the perils of travel. Other than a brief wherry trip to Lausanne during my studies, I had never left the city.

From the city's stench to the lake's fishy scent, I braced myself for a far worse olfactory assault, as there was no way to avoid the tanners. No way unless, of course, I traversed the plague cemetery and the plague hospital. I did not want to face that—I needed to remain focused. Truly, I prefer the smell of human excrement to the foul odors emanating from the tanning area along the river. It is no wonder many plague workers come from tanning families—exchanging one foulness for another.

By mid-morning, the city was behind me, the Rhone had widened to a reedy expanse, and I was enjoying the scent of fresh air and the last of the year's crickets and birdsong. At the Peney crossroads, I tied up my horse and stopped to eat. I was lucky to have spotted the small carved stone at all; had I missed it, I would have found myself in Savoy and, in my black Protestant robes, the uniform of Geneva and the Reformed faith, truly in the mouths of lions.

After lunch, I turned into the forest to follow the stream known as Nant d'Avril that would take me to Satigny. The horse's hooves crunched as the first autumn leaves swirled gently around us, and the wind whistled through the trees. The forest was so thick that I was completely disoriented and couldn't decide whether the whispering trees were beautiful or ominous. But there was no doubt that the stream was truly beautiful. And plentiful, too: at intervals, the stream would form minuscule waterfalls into pools of an ethereal opaque blue that were filled with spawning trout. The rolling incline of the forest was so dramatic I almost felt the ground moving as if I was on a boat. How could it have been there all this time while I had no idea?

I chose a flat, stony beach to stop for the horse and me to drink. I thought I had to be close to the village by then. It was the farthest I had been from Geneva in many years, and I must confess I was anxious. I scooped up my robes to bend and...realized I was not alone. A woven basket lay on the stones some way from my position. At first, I thought perhaps there was a baby inside because it was moving, rocking slightly. I let go of my bridle and moved cautiously towards the basket, only to see it was filled with fish, some of which were frantically flapping as they took their last gasps. I looked around to see who the owner might be. And then I saw her.

With another basket under one arm, she stood on a rocky ledge above me, her skirts hiked up so I could see white ankles and calf muscles. She had not noticed me and was pulling at some root, having clambered animal-like to reach it. When she pulled it out, the momentum almost knocked her onto her back, and when I saw her smile at herself at her clumsiness, I smiled too. Someone who, like me, enjoyed their own company. She sniffed at the root, closing her eyes in satisfaction, and placed it carefully in the basket filled with other plants, flowers, and berries.

My horse shook its mane with a loud shudder.

The woman gasped and stood to her full height. Her skirts fell back to her ankles. She wore a simple brown linen tunic with an apron—a poor woman—but there was something regal about her, nevertheless. Her cap covered most of her head, but I could see that her hair was long and light brown. Her face was angular and beautiful, and she looked quite young. Perhaps the same age as me.

As soon as I glanced at her, the sun moved, blinding me through branches and obscuring her features. All I could see was her silhouette. She bowed her head, curtseyed slightly, and remained bowed—an odd position since I was so far below her. She did not move from her modest stoop, so there was nothing for me to do but take my horse and go. As I turned to leave, I noticed tiny red movements around her —she was surrounded by squirrels. One leaped playfully onto her shoulder, the silhouette of its ears like tufted horns.

I mounted and rode on, swifter than before, disconcerted in a way I couldn't quite define. What was a young woman doing alone in the forest? Those squirrels! Almost like familiar spirits. Perhaps I should have done something differently—said something, helped her down, handed her the basket of fish, asked for directions. Why can I never say or do the right thing, no matter how much I think about it? But no, it would not have been appropriate. And I have never been skilled at talking to women. In truth, I have hardly ever spoken to them. The fear of being seduced, my mind or body poisoned—the risks are great. I touched the bag with the *Malleus* and reminded myself of the treachery of women.

Soon after, I emerged from the trees into the hamlet of Peney. I could see what Calvin had meant about the wealth in those fields; vineyards stretched in all directions, rolling gently with the curves of the land, gnarled vine trees neatly ranged and pregnant with grapes. The vineyards were occasionally broken by an apple orchard or a field of cabbages, but there were signs of plenty everywhere. How the poor from within the city walls would descend on that fresh food.

I knew it was a sparsely populated area but even so, it was eerily quiet for a fine mid-afternoon. At harvest time, surely the fields should be filled with people picking grapes, scything corn, or whatever it is they do in rural areas. Instead, there was a silence, or not quite—the wind had whipped up slightly, whistling through the corn fields like the voices of a thousand ghosts. Had the place been so decimated by the plague that, unlike the city, it had no live bodies to spare? I suddenly had the feeling of being the only person alive on this Earth, and it was terrible.

As I neared the cluster of buildings that was surely the village center, the only sound was the breeze. Corpses hung from the gallows at the entrance to the village square—a man and a woman. I wondered whether their crimes had been committed together—adultery perhaps. Or perhaps they were a reminder that the city's poor would be wise not to try their luck finding free nourishment in the fields. Unlike the executed bodies in Geneva, which had been still and hooded, these two swung wildly in the wind as if they were dancing, and their faces were visible in all their horror. Three out of four eyeballs had already been plucked out by birds. It was truly a ghost village.

But how foolish I was—bells rang, and when my eyes followed my ears up to the steeple on top of a hill around half a mile away, I saw groups shuffling up the hill and into the church. Of course, it was Wednesday afternoon, and churchgoing had become compulsory now, as on Sundays, for every citizen of Geneva and its *mandements*. It would be a perfect opportunity to observe the citizens in close quarters and since I had not had time to make any arrangements, including lodgings, it would also be an opportunity to seek out the *châtelain* Donzel.

As I rode up Peney Hill to the church, the horse was forced to maneuver past the rubble of the fallen Chateau de Peney. Less than ten years ago, the castle had been filled with rebels—heretics and Savoyard nobles—but Genevan troops, assisted by Berne, had broken their siege, destroyed them all, and brought wavering villages such as Satigny into line. There was no denying the poignancy of the once-proud fortress reduced to crumbling walls and moss. But the chapel stood proud as a bastion of the true church, a phoenix rising from the ashes of hypocrisy and the false promises of popery.

There was only just enough room for me to secure the horse at the water trough next to several other beasts no doubt owned by the *châtelain* and the area's wealthier farmers. I eased the church door open as quietly as possible, but its creaking and my footsteps on the stones caused no small number of heads to turn. There were no spaces amongst the pews, so I leaned against the back wall, a perfect vantage point to take in my surroundings.

Men on one side, women on the other. I estimated two hundred people altogether and that it must have been the whole of the population of the village, save for any prisoners or madmen, since attendance is compulsory. Many of the men were proudly holding Bibles, studying them, and nodding along with the pastor's words, and I noticed with a smile that some were holding them upside down.

Having been brought up listening to the great Viret, Farel, and of course, Calvin himself, I have very high standards for my religious teachers. But I had to admit that the pastor was excellent. The old church had been suitably whitewashed, cleansed of any idolatry, so all attention was on the pastor's words, but I imagined he could have held it amidst any distractions. He was a diminutive figure, small, slight, and clean-shaven, with the plain black robes all clergy now wear, yet an aura of profound gentleness that somehow transcended his stature. He exuded a kindness and hope that almost brought tears to my eyes and made me wonder how there could be such evil in the village. He was using the Genevan psalter, of course, and I recognized direct quotations from Calvin's sermons. Taking in every face of the congregation, the pastor said, "We should ask God to increase our hope when it is small, awaken it when it is dormant, confirm it when it is wavering, strengthen it when it is weak, and raise it up when it is overthrown. There is not one blade of grass; there is no color in this world that is not intended to make us rejoice."

I wondered which smiling people were imbued with the spirit of the Devil. Which amongst those women had committed those vile acts. Which among the villagers knew I was the magistrate sent to judge them. I had a sudden inkling of my power over them, and I stood a little taller with the importance of my mission.

"And now, we shall sing," the pastor announced, and there was a rustling of pages and a shuffling of bodies. The singing was a poor, tentative cacophony compared to the heavenly plainsong at the Cathedral of St. Pierre. But there was no doubt that the pastor was leading his flock safely down the path of the Reformed faith. I cast my eyes across the backs of the women's heads, wondering whether she was there. Most of them wore similar white bonnets, but I strongly sensed she was not present. Perhaps she belonged to another of the villages in the Satigny *mandement*. And yet the stream where I saw her had been so close to the church. Who would dare miss the Wednesday church service?

⚜

As the congregation filed out, I decided to stay at the back of the church to observe the villagers. Many of them looked at me and whispered, and I felt a mixture of self-consciousness and power.

Their dress was different from that in the city. Most were agricultural workers wearing simple smocks and linens, even in what I imagined must be their best for church. There was less difference between rich and poor than in the city. The new fashions for Spanish lace and puffed, slit sleeves had not yet arrived, and the wealthier women, who I assumed were the landowning farmers' wives, wore autumn-colored velvets with simple adornments. I saw them looking up and down at my black robes and my person. I have always tried to blend into the background of things and have a very unassuming manner but a slightly less unassuming physical presence due to my height.

When the church was nearly empty, I was about to go to the front and introduce myself to the pastor tidying the altar. But my path up the aisle was blocked by a red-faced, portly gentleman who thrust his hand out. He was more extravagantly dressed than anyone I had seen in the city itself, with yellow velvet breeches and matching exaggerated sleeves to his doublet, all slashed to reveal green silk underneath. His codpiece, an English affectation rarely seen in Geneva, was also exaggerated and thrust towards me so that its closeness was an affront. His beard was impeccably—almost absurdly—groomed, and his eyes sparkled with perpetual amusement.

"Henry Aubert, our magistrate, I believe. Jean-Philippe Donzel, *châtelain* of Satigny. They told me we were getting a new fellow, but, in the name of God, you are younger than I expected." He had maintained a painfully firm grip on my hand and clasped my arm with the other, shaking me vigorously, his chuckles resonating in the church rafters. Without letting go, he roared over his shoulder, "Look at this young upstart they have sent us!"

The pastor glided down the aisle, and I was finally released from Donzel's grip.

"Jacques Bernard, pastor of Peney. Thank you for coming to our assistance, Monsieur Aubert. We are honored to have sparked the interest of our savior, Calvin."

"Thank you, I am honored to serve you. Tell me, as I may have to stay for some time, do you know where I might be lodging?" Again, it was odd to hear the sound of my own voice, as if I conversed with strangers all the time.

"Peney Inn is the only place, and you'll find its rooms comfortable. Particularly if Rolette's daughter comes knocking in the night," said Donzel.

"Rolette?"

"The landlady and her daughter have been known to offer...extra services on occasion."

Bernard coughed awkwardly. "Please ignore *Monsieur le châtelain*. We are working towards Calvin's godly society here in Satigny, and I'm sure you will find our people well-behaved."

"Yes, yes," said Donzel dismissively, ushering me out of the church. "Anyway, you'll take your life in your hands eating Rolette's food today —I know for a fact the chicken soup steaming in her hearth has been festering there for a week. You must dine with me. You too, pastor, for we have much to discuss. We thought there would be a reprieve from the terrible year our *mandement* has had, and now we find ourselves thrust again into the fray."

As Donzel's and my horses picked their way down Peney Hill, the pastor walked beside us, the sunset bathing the sky in pink and purple. With the steep foothills of the Jura to our left, barred from us by thick forest, I again had a curious sense of unreality, of being in a liminal space on the edge of the world.

We passed through the village square, where a woman was trapped in the pillory. She moaned weakly but appeared to bear her punishment for whatever she had done with acceptance. She looked cold, and I wondered whether someone would come and release her before sundown. A stench of urine, horse shit, and rotten vegetables emanated from her vicinity. To my horror, as we rode by, Donzel dismounted and, without even breaking his conversation, unbuttoned his breeches and urinated on her. As if it was nothing at all. For some reason, I desperately wanted to watch, and it was hard to tear my eyes away, but Bernard awkwardly averted his until it was over, and I felt I should join him.

But it was exciting, the humiliation of it—why did it enthrall me so much? I had never seen such a spectacle, and I wanted to think about it but was forced to snap myself back into the moment. I resolved to reconsider it at length later in the evening when I was alone.

Sitting just past the square, Donzel's house is the largest and grandest in the village. It is similar in style to the finest in the city, except lower—a two-story square house with a handsome corner tower. Donzel promised to show me his vaulted wine caves after dinner. We were soon seated at his table, his wife and housekeeper serving us a delicious meal with the finest, freshest meat I had tasted in a long time.

Donzel began to pour me some wine from a flagon in the center of the table.

"Oh no, thank you. I don't partake when I'm working."

"Come now, work can start tomorrow. This is wine country. And I know for a fact that the great John Calvin is partial to a glass of wine or three with dinner."

I smarted at the slight sarcasm with which he said 'the great' Calvin. What did he mean?

"Very well, thank you." I had to admit it was excellent wine, and I began to relax.

I asked him to tell me a little more about the case for which I had been called under such exceptional circumstances.

"Martine Folliez. Wife of Guillaume Folliez, the most prosperous farmer in the area. She has accused her lying-in maid of killing her child by witchcraft—an unbaptized baby, too, six weeks old. The maid, Susanne Darnex, is currently in Satigny prison with her husband and has accused all and sundry—four definite names so far. Every time we go in there, she spouts someone else's. If we are to take them seriously, we cannot cope with four arrests. And no doubt there will be more. We need to root them all out."

Bernard had been shifting uncomfortably the whole time. "Remember, Monsieur Donzel, much of this is gossip."

Donzel laughed. "Gossip, witchcraft, they are one and the same."

At that, Bernard slammed down his drink so the table shook slightly. "In God's name, they are not the same! We need to know the difference. These are people's lives!"

"They are women's lives, *mon curé,*" said Donzel. He turned to me. "Look here, women accuse each other all the time, you know, petty squabbles and suchlike. It's an opportunity to bring them into line and get rid of some of the unruly widows. They're useless, a drain on society."

Bernard sighed. "Look here, Monsieur Aubert, I do believe there is evil in this village. So many bad things have happened. So many people have died. The Devil is knocking on the door. Evil does exist, and it is everywhere. And to deny that, I suppose, would be heresy."

I agreed with him completely and nodded. "We must distinguish rumor from true evil. There must be due legal process, and that is my job."

"The problem with this village, Henry," Donzel said through a mouthful of roast chicken that dripped juices down his chin, "is there are too many unsupervised women."

"The war left many widows," said Bernard, trying to elevate the conversation again. "Plague, too, of course. If a man's wife dies, he can simply remarry, whatever his age. For a woman, it is not so straight-forward."

Donzel swung out his glass for his wife to refill, and she appeared dutifully.

"It is not the natural order of things, having all these women running around." At this, Donzel slapped his wife's behind, and she retaliated with a shove—angry or playful, I could not tell—that sloshed his wine.

Embarrassed, I turned to Bernard. It was surely time for me to contribute something, so I asked him a question. "Are you married, Pastor?"

"Not yet, but I hope to be one day. As our *châtelain* says, the marital state is the natural order of things. And you, sir?"

"No, not yet."

Donzel laughed. "Then I'll wager you're missing all those city whorehouses and bathhouses that it has pleased Calvin to close down."

I decided to ignore him. "I understand one of the accused is a man."

"The husband of the lying-in maid." Donzel nodded, rolling his eyes. "Witches often rope them in. We have only those two in custody so far, but she is raving about all sorts of names. That's why we need you here. The village can't cope—apart from everything else, we only have two prison cells. I'll bring you to see her tomorrow."

"Where is she kept?"

"At the Satigny prison."

"I'd like to start with her accuser."

"Of course. We will go to the Folliez house first."

They talked about village matters for a while—grain stocks, the best day for the wine harvest—and I was conscious of my silence. I thought for a long time about what I might say; I had several ideas and opened my mouth to speak a few times, but I could not find the right moment. And, in any case, my mind was filled with thoughts of the urination incident with the woman in the stocks and of the beauty of the woman in the forest.

"Tell me," I said, apropos of nothing, concentrating on cleaning my knife with the edge of my fork, "was the whole village in attendance at today's service? Other than the woman in the stocks?"

Donzel spat out his wine, laughing. "You should have joined me in having a good piss on her. But I suppose, in those robes of yours, it's not so easy. I hear that, in England, they use an iron mask on women like her. A scold's bridle, they call it. But this is much more fun. I have threatened Prudence with it many a time."

At this, his wife, who had been clearing out plates, shot him daggers. It seemed to me she had more control over him than he liked to admit.

"We are very vigilant, sir. We have watchers. Everyone attends, as is compulsory," said Bernard.

I could see he was nervous, being questioned by an envoy from the city. It made me proud to be Calvin's representative. I must remember that I have power over these people. "I see. It's just that I saw a woman alone in the forest just outside the village, and she was not in church. Perhaps she belongs to another village within the *mandement*?" I continued eating, eager to disguise my interest in her.

But Bernard and Donzel looked at each other. "Young and fair, was she? With a basket?"

I nodded.

"That will be Louise de Peney," said Donzel. "She gets something of a free pass, an occasional exception on Wednesdays, at least, if she is busy with someone sick or with child."

I noticed that even Donzel softened his attitude when it came to that woman. "Louise de Peney? She is a noblewoman, then? That sounds like the name of a landed family."

Donzel nodded. "Well, in a manner of speaking. She was the third daughter of the de Peney family, sent to a convent at a very young age. What a curse to have borne three daughters. When the Poor Clares was closed, she returned to the village. Her sister and husband were living in the family seat—a very nice house out past the inn, and they took her in. Rather unwillingly, I might add, but she proved herself quite useful."

"Wait. Was she a Poor Clare? A Clarisse? It is not possible that she could be here. They were all moved to Annecy. That is, all but those who chose to take husbands."

The convent of the Poor Clares was opposite my house—the building itself is still there, converted into the city hospital. I was there ten years ago, the day the remaining nuns were escorted from Geneva under armed guard—protecting them or threatening them, it was not clear. The whole city turned out to watch, and there were so many tears. Even to those like me, filled with the fervor of the reformed faith, it felt like the last bastion of the old faith had finally crumbled. I remember how windy it was, and how their habits swirled around them as their tragic procession huddled over the bridge in pairs.

"Not all, it seems," said Bernard. "Louise escaped her escort. Only God knows how with all those guards and the whole city watching—it was a miracle—and found her way home. The entire de Peney family died in the plague of 1540, but she survived and has lived alone ever since. It is odd for her to occupy that large house all alone—odd and perhaps even dangerous—but she has proved so useful to our and the surrounding villages that she is left in peace."

"That or everyone's bloody terrified of her," said Donzel. "Have you seen the squirrels? Familiars if ever I saw—"

"Useful how?" I hoped I did not sound too interested.

"She is a healer. A cunning woman, you know."

"A healer? Then she is using magic?? That is heresy! St. Augustine condemns all forms of magic as paganism and heresy. What is going on here?"

"Healing is perhaps not the right word," said Bernard, placating me. "She is more of a doctor. We don't have hospitals or apothecary shops out here, you know—our ways are different. She received an impressive education at the Convent of the Poor Clares, and apparently many women of the city came to her during their pregnancies and lying-in times. She is certainly the only woman in this village who knows how to read and write. Not many of the men do yet either, I must admit."

"Why has she not married? She must have had no shortage of suitors..."

Donzel and Bernard did not appear to have a satisfactory answer and lapsed into a conversation about people I didn't know. I cursed myself for hinting at my interest again. I thought of her basket, of how expertly she searched for that root—no doubt for some medicine or other. If I were a healer, I would be tempted to keep that knowledge to myself. Nobody thanks a healer when they succeed, yet they are terribly vulnerable in failure.

I have never been skilled at conversation. I am in my element within the structure of my work—an investigation or a trial with a prescribed format, a script. I can hardly remember my last social occasion—except perhaps the meeting with Calvin, if one can count that as social—and I was finding it exhausting. How to listen while thinking of the next thing to say? That is a skill I have never had the chance to master. I wanted to be alone with my thoughts. Moreover, I was physically exhausted after the day's ride and my lack of sleep the night before.

I agonized for a while over how to select the moment, then rose, I hope not too abruptly. "Well, gentlemen, perhaps I shall retire. If you can point me in the direction of the inn."

They rose too, and Donzel directed me across the village square, informing me that he had sent word for Madame Rolette to prepare her finest room for me. But my heart sank when I entered the inn. I don't know what I was expecting, as I had never visited an inn or public house of any kind. But, even at that late hour, the place was filled with people. Nothing particularly untoward that I saw but loud voices laughing, singing.

Donzel left me in the doorway, signaling my arrival to a large woman behind the bar dressed as colorfully as him.

"Well, see you tomorrow, magistrate." With that, he shook my hand and left.

Despite his boorish manners, I felt adrift without him. I had to weave between the bodies to get to the bar, then raise my voice to be heard by Madame Rolette. I was relieved not to see any dancing; I know for a fact that the council is planning to ban dancing very soon. This village needs to be brought into line and, as Calvin said, this is a perfect opportunity.

I imagined myself as a city elder in a few years, regal and gowned, holding court in the Consistory, pronouncing on the minutiae of people's lives. It was an excellent thought, and I resolved to add it to my arsenal of imaginings.

My room is at the top of a narrow, creaky staircase behind the bar and, although it smells a little damp, it is clean, warm, and spacious. I locked the door with the iron key Madame Rolette had given me, and leaned against it to survey my surroundings, exhausted. I realized, with a certain amount of exhilaration, that I had touched door handles, strangers' plates and glasses—strangers' hands! How the ground had shifted beneath me in only a few hours. I felt drunk with it all—and wondered if perhaps I was.

The bed is reasonably comfortable, but sleep will not come, so I write by candlelight. I am disturbed by the unfamiliar noises of the countryside—an owl hooting, a smattering of late summer crickets— and the noises of the inn. The merry voices reached a peak at some point when they bustled out into the square outside and, I imagined, dispersed to their homes. But then there were other noises from inside the inn's rooms; moaning and grunting, sounds I did not recognize. Perhaps ghosts. At one point, I thought I heard a soft knocking on the door. I remembered what Donzel had said about Rolette's daughter, but now I am finally drifting on the edges of sleep, so I will pull the covers up against myself and against her intrusion into my solitude.

❧ 4 ❧

MANUM MISI IN IGNEM

SEPTEMBER 8, 1545

In the morning, I awoke to a strange sound—an angry sort of rhythmic cawing and cackling—and my first thought was that a whole coven of witches had gathered outside the inn. I looked out the window to see fields bathed in white mist and dotted with large black birds diving in and out of the mist or settled on treetops. Rooks. I had, of course, seen them in the city, but had never been so aware of their strange otherworldly call amidst the background noise of the city. Again, I had this curious sense of being on the edge of the world.

I cannot deny that I breakfasted well. Not since my childhood had I had food provided for me. Next to a roaring fire downstairs, Madame Rolette served me excellent ale—better than anything I had tasted in the city—with bread, cheese, sausage, and grapes. Everything smells better here, and the air is fresh.

Unfortunately, however, Madame Rolette could not bring herself to leave me to enjoy my breakfast in peace. She asked incessant questions about the case and mentioned her daughter Pernette so often that I soon realized, with dismay, that she must be planning to foist the girl on me. As if that could possibly be a suitable match!

Pernette herself eventually emerged—her mother had clearly been stalling while she prepared herself. She had evidently dressed to look as she imagined city girls dress. She had added puffed sleeves and a farthingale to her simple peasant dress, and slashed the neckline low to reveal her bosom. An attempt had been made to imitate the new Spanish lace with complicated black stitching on her bodice, but it looked like a child's spindly writing. She had put white lead and rouge on her face, added flowers to her cap, and was draping herself around the bar, moving in a strange manner I assume was intended to display her figure from different angles. It would have been endearing if it wasn't so mortifying. To the women's disappointment, I left moments after Pernette emerged.

I set out for Donzel's house, where he was ready to mount his horse. He wore an outfit even more outlandish than the previous one, all red and purple satins with exaggerated puffed sleeves and a large white ruff. He appeared to be aiming for as wide a silhouette as possible, in complete contrast to the city pronouncements for simple, form-fitting dark materials. We made the short journey across the fields to the Folliez farm. The fields were busy; with harvest time approaching, the vines were rich with plump bunches of grapes, while the apple trees bulged with fruit. A corn field was populated by two lines: first, men scything the corn, followed by women—some with babies strapped to their backs—collecting the ears.

The Folliez farmhouse is one of the finest in the village but, like so many others, it is steeped in sadness. Plague may be slightly easier to escape in the countryside, away from our overcrowding, but the dangers of childbirth and childhood do not distinguish between rich and poor. The door was opened by a tiny housemaid, who must have been no more than twelve years old, and we were shown into a drawing room less fashionable, but much larger than those in grand city houses.

A tall, regal-looking woman entered, wearing an elegant dress of fine black cloth overlaid with lace. She was pale with grief and grim with determination.

Donzel introduced us. "Magistrate, this is Madame Folliez, whose baby died in suspicious circumstances not two weeks ago."

I managed to murmur my condolences, but then hesitated and we stood in an awkward circle, because in truth, I had never conducted an interview of any kind.

"Shall we begin?" Donzel clapped his hands together and motioned for us to sit down, but I realized that I must be the one to take control of the situation.

So, with as much authority as I could muster, I said, "In fact, Monsieur le châtelain, I would speak to the lady alone."

Perhaps it was a little too abrupt, as both Donzel and Madame Folliez both halted mid-stoop on their way to sit down.

"Suit yourself." Donzel hovered for a moment, indignant, then left the room.

I am no stranger to homes beset by grief. None of us are. There are few that do not exist under a near-permanent cloud of misery in these times. Children die much more frequently than adults, but surely mankind will never get used to it. The moment we accept it is the moment we lose our humanity. Our great consolation is that it is God's will and, in His mysterious ways, His will be done.

But I was at the Folliez house as a magistrate. Not to console, but to investigate. Fully aware that it was the first time I had investigated anything by myself, I felt the thrill of being on the brink of something, of making it up as I went along. Until now, I have always been an assistant, a junior, but I can look upon this as my playground.

"Madame Folliez, you have accused Susanne Darnex, your lying-in maid, of using witchcraft to kill your child. Tell me more about what happened."

She stared into the distance, as if searching for the strength to speak. For once it was I who had to fill the silence.

"I understand he was not yet baptized?"

She nodded, and we both shuddered.

This piece of information had struck terror into my heart. There can be few fates more terrible than that of an unbaptized baby, cast into Hell, forever a demon in Satan's army. And it is well known that witches target unbaptized children.

"When did you suspect Madame Darnex?"

"She came into my employment at the beginning of my confinement. It was perfect; her own baby had just died, so her milk was plentiful; her husband's crop had failed, and they needed the money. Now, I wonder how indeed that baby died, and how indeed that crop failed."

I did wonder momentarily at her apparent callousness, the way she spoke of the convenience of a baby's death. But then, I suppose, that is the way of things—how else were wetnurses produced? And then, the woman's own baby had died, possibly at the maid's hands, so she could be forgiven for her callousness. If the maid in question was indeed a witch, then maybe the crop failure was linked to her after all.

"Did she live here with you for the duration of her time?"

"Yes, of course—that is how it works, sir. She slept in the room with the baby. Occasionally, she would go back to her own house during the daytime."

"And was she attentive to the baby? To you?"

The woman hesitated for a moment, then her face hardened. "Too attentive, I would say. She loved that baby too much, as if he were a replacement for her own. During my six weeks of confinement, visitors would say how wonderful she was, how happily the baby looked at her, how well she fed him. How lucky I was to have found such a wonderful maid, how I should keep her."

As she spoke, Monsieur Folliez entered the room, and I stood to make his acquaintance. He was a gentleman farmer, dressed not in a dirty smock like his laborers, but in a smart jerkin and hose and a feathered cap. He stood behind his wife, a comforting hand on her shoulder, but his words were less comforting. "There were some elements of jealousy, shall we say."

"Oh, do shut up," she snapped, brushing his hand away. "How can you possibly understand what it's like as a woman to be stripped of her dignity, bleeding and shitting and pissing from every orifice..."

Both the husband and I blushed and looked away at the unwelcome details.

The woman was clearly not in her right mind to be so vulgar. She continued. "Trapped in bed at the mercy of a pretty young thing who is free to flirt with your husband. Don't think I didn't hear you giggling together in the kitchen."

"Did she keep the baby from you, madame?" I asked.

"No, she brought the baby to me often, but I believe she had severed the connection between us. That baby looked at me as if I were nothing. Worse—he hated my breast, fussed and cried. And I had but a trickle of milk. It only seemed to flow while I was lying there watching her feed my child, cooing and making eyes..."

"When did you begin to suspect her of witchcraft?"

"I suspected nothing, until afterwards. Fool that I am. But things changed at around five weeks, when I told her that her services would no longer be required after six weeks. That is the normal time, you know. After my coming out ceremony at church. She took it very badly. She begged to stay longer—for the sake of the child, she said. How dare she suggest that I could not feed my own child? I must admit I slapped her hard. After that, she became meek again, and indeed, she became quite attentive to me. She began bringing me soups and herbal teas to help increase my milk—I didn't have very much, you see—and she would watch the baby anxiously at my breast, and then take her to feed her again afterwards. It was infuriating, because when she was hovering, the baby became fussy, distracted by her, so I became angry with both of them. I knew that this baby would never nurse properly until she was out of the house. The day came, and she left in floods of tears and dramatics. I was so filled with relief I cannot tell you."

"And when did your baby become sick?"

"This was no ordinary sickness, sir. I watched my baby turn into a shriveled monster. He rejected me, he screamed constantly, his excrement was foul green froth, he bit at the breast like a tiny demon. My breasts turned purple and rotten, and it felt as if a thousand tiny swords attacked them. Within days, his skin had turned gray and veined purple, his cries became shrieks, and then whimpers, and then he just... faded away."

"Madame, why do you believe it was her?"

"I do not believe, I know. As sure as God is in Heaven and Satan is on his throne in Hell, she poisoned my milk with those herbs and potions. And they came from her own garden, from their farm, so it was him as well. They needed my unbaptized child as an offering to the Devil, in return for a good harvest. And you shall see, his crops will make a miraculous recovery in time for it."

I stood to take my leave. "Madame, thank you for your time. I will investigate this and do my utmost to help speed God's divine justice."

She looked at me with eyes so pale and devoid of... of what, I don't know. I am so unpracticed in the art of reading people.

❧

Donzel waited for me outside and, although I would not have known the way to the prison without him, I could tell that his constant presence during the mission was going to irritate me. I tried to ride in front, but he hurried his horse up alongside me.

"You know, there's a quarrel between the husbands too."

"How so?"

"Darnex works Folliez's fields and hasn't pulled his weight since his own child died. He's convinced that Folliez has been trying to seduce his wife, with them living in such close quarters. And he probably wasn't wrong either—I mean who wouldn't, eh?" He gave me a friendly slap on the arm, from which I instinctively recoiled.

He didn't notice. "But with Darnex shouting his mouth off and damaging the farmer's reputation, accusing him as well is a chance to get rid of them both at once."

"So, you think this is just gossip and rumor?"

"Rumor is the central tenet of a witchcraft investigation, man! Have they taught you nothing?"

I didn't answer. It felt like a rhetorical question, although I didn't know for sure. And, in any case, I was preoccupied.

After a while he said, "You don't talk much, do you?" He slapped me on the back.

Still, I didn't answer, lost in the fearful thought that I might be about to meet a real witch.

Donzel said, in a very different voice, "No, I do not talk to lowly village people. Don't you know I am city magistrate and a witch hunter sent by Calvin himself?"

I think he intended to be comical, but I had no reply.

Eventually, he uttered a sound I didn't understand and ushered his horse on ahead.

We rode to the prison of Satigny, the largest village in the *mande-ment* and the only place prisoners could be held securely since the destruction of Peney Castle. I scanned the fields idly on the way, wondering if I might catch a glimpse of this Louise de Peney, wondering if she might be part of the reaper teams. By the time we arrived at the tiny, crumbling stone fortress that was Satigny prison, Donzel seemed to have forgiven me whatever mistake I had made.

"Here we are, my legal friend." He slapped me on the back again. "Come inside, I think you'll find I have prepared the prisoners well for you. We have six guards who work in shifts, so the place is well attended." He motioned to two halberd-bearing men in full blue and yellow livery, who had scrambled to attention on our approach.

"How long have they been..." I began but, as we entered the prison, I was hit with a multisensory assault. The stench of excrement, and the sound of ghostly moaning, sometimes punctuated by clanking metal on stone, of struggle, sometimes punctuated by plaintive and angry cries.

There was a little daylight coming from the window grilles next to the ceiling, and my eyes gradually became accustomed to the dark. I saw two cells only divided up to waist level, although there was no chance of the two prisoners being able to move towards each other. In the cell to my left, a woman was kneeling, one foot awkwardly turned out to the side, as it was clamped in irons attached to the wall. Her face was thrust up to the ceiling as if in prayer. But it was not voluntary prayer. There was an iron collar around her neck with a pair of two-pronged forks at the front, one piercing her chin and forcing her neck upwards at an unnatural angle, the other piercing her chest just enough to be embedded in her skin, creating two trickles of crusted blood. Her voice box was quivering, and her breathing was clearly labored. In the cell to my right was a man in exactly the same position. His pronounced Adam's apple was crushed against the back of the fork, and his breathing was even more labored.

The Heretic's Fork. I had heard of the device but never seen it used. The Spanish Inquisition wished to force heretics to face the God they had betrayed, as they slowly choked to death over a period of agonizing days.

"What the Devil is going on here? Who gave you authority to do this?"

"I don't need your authority, sir. You may be from the city, but don't forget that we were administering justice here long before you arrived."

"But what made you choose the Heretic's Fork?"

"As we all know, witchcraft is heresy. I have read the book too, you know." He nodded to the *Malleus* I was clutching.

"But they have not yet been convicted—"

"And your book also says that you're much more likely to secure a conviction if you soften the prisoners up before interrogation."

I could not deny that Donzel was more experienced than me in such matters. Worse, he knew it, and he knew that I knew it too. He was going to stay and enjoy the show, and there was nothing I could do to stop him; indeed, I needed him as a witness. I was going to have to find my mettle and show him I was not afraid to do what was necessary.

I instructed the guards to release them from the contraptions and give them something to eat.

"Where can I question them?" I asked Donzel. "I can't see a thing in here."

"This is it, I'm afraid. We will bring candles, torches, and a chair for you, magistrate."

I decided to begin with the husband. For some reason, I felt more confident questioning a man, and I had also heard that men break much faster than women, so perhaps I could get it over with quickly. I was suddenly very tired. I had a strange feeling of desperately not wanting to be there, of wanting to be just about anywhere else. I was sinking into something, utterly out of my depth. It was intolerable to question a suspect in that hole, where he sat in his own excrement. But I couldn't see an alternative, other than taking him out into the light and in the view of other villagers. The whole enterprise was enough of a spectacle already.

So, I found myself sitting on a stool in the middle of the cell with the forlorn figure of Amyed Darnex slumped against the wall in front of me, his legs splayed like a child. I almost felt as if I were the one on trial. The guards had placed torches in the iron sconces around the room so I could see my notes, and the flames lit the contours of our faces. Donzel and a guard watched from behind the bars. I cleared my throat and read the beginning of the script that I had prepared from my notebook.

"Monsieur Darnex, you have been accused of *sorcellerie*, of causing the death of the baby Folliez, of making a potion, with your wife, to possess and kill an unbaptized baby to consecrate him to the Devil. What say you to the charges?"

He did not reply, only stared into space, nursing his sore throat and neck.

"Monsieur Darnex, did you hear me?" I repeated the charges, feeling my own neck redden and my body overheat as Donzel snorted from the sidelines. "Monsieur Darnex?"

Slowly, he turned to face me. "I am innocent."

I could barely hear him, so weak was his voice. "Can you repeat that please?"

"I am innocent." He had tried to raise his voice, but the pain was too great, and he erupted into a coughing fit.

I waited, squirming inside.

From the next cell, his wife called weakly, "I am here, Amyed, I am here."

I tried to ignore her. "Monsieur Darnex, have you ever conversed with a demon?"

He shook his head. "I have not."

"Have you ever attended a witches' Sabbath?"

"I have not."

"Have you ever pledged allegiance to the Devil?"

"I have not."

It was hopeless. We continued in that way for some time and, as Donzel had warned, Darnex gave me nothing. No admission of involvement, no names, nothing I could use at all. He struggled to speak, in fact, so damaged was his throat by that damned Heretic's Fork. I realized the wife was far feistier. Several times, I had to yell at her to be quiet as she interrupted my interrogation with her shouting.

Eventually, Donzel approached the bars and beckoned me over. He whispered, "If you want to get anything out of him, you're going to have to move on to other methods."

"What do you have here?"

"Well, we don't have a strappado here—at least, not since it pleased the city to destroy our castle." He laughed and slapped me on the back through the bars, and I wondered how many times he was going to do that.

But he was right; my only option was to move on to torture and, with Donzel watching from the corridor in a state of barely concealed glee, I had to think fast. With little at my disposal, I improvised. "Guard, can you bring me some firewood, stones, and tongs from the blacksmith?"

Moments later, I could hear shouts outside—the guard asking a boy from the gathered crowd to go procure these items. There was no disguising my intentions, and I immediately regretted the idea but, with Donzel watching, there was no going back. It was an interminable wait for the boy to return, and unbearable to be in there with the prisoners, so I went outside and sat on a rock. I pretended to study my notes, frequently searching the horizon until finally the boy came struggling back, laden with my equipment.

While I was making the fire, on which I placed several smooth, round stones the boy had brought, Darnex was relatively calm; perhaps he had not realized the significance of the tongs.

I had seen feet heating done before, in plague-spreading trials. It is considered a mild form of torture. Thinking about it now, I can hardly believe I did it. I felt dizzy, bewitched—perhaps I was bewitched. I used the tongs to pick a hot stone from the flames, dropping it a couple of times before I got a firm grip. I stood in front of Darnex and said, "Monsieur Darnex, I will ask you again, have you ever renounced God and pledged allegiance to the Devil?"

As I raised the tongs and the stone glowed orange, I felt a rush of —what? Ecstasy? Power, certainly. I was emboldened with a curious recklessness, and it was intoxicating. And I wished he was a woman, and I was alone with that power, without a crowd judging me outside.

Darnex looked from me to the tongs in disbelief, and instinctively shrank back, but there was nowhere to go. He said nothing, open-mouthed, so I thrust the stone against the sole of his foot and held it there. After a momentary pause, the pain hit and he screamed, and again I felt that delicious rush of excitement. How strange a feeling it was.

But, amidst his screams, I became aware of Donzel shouting too, having approached the iron bars. "Good God, man, you moved too soon! You have to show him the instrument first! Threaten him with it, see if he caves! Have they taught you nothing?"

In truth, no, they had not. And there was another problem; I had forgotten that, when I had seen feet heating, the subject's legs had been immobilized in a wooden chair designed for that. But Darnex's were free to move, and he hid them underneath himself. Should I burn him somewhere else on his body? I had no idea. "Guard, you must hold his legs!" I called, and the guard looked uncertainly at Donzel, who nodded for him to enter the cell.

The guard forced Donzel's legs straight and lay across them as I took a fresh stone from the fire and raised the tongs again.

"Monsieur Darnex, have you ever renounced God and pledged allegiance to the Devil?"

I was supposed to wait for a reply, but something drove me forward and I plunged the tongs into position on his other foot, holding them there as the flesh hissed and sizzled. That strange excitement I had had dissipated and this time, it was more horrible than exhilarating. But the desired result was achieved, because he confessed.

"Yes, yes, I renounced God. I do renounce Him." Wide-eyed and nodding, Darnex looked as if he had just remembered something. "I pledged allegiance to the Devil! Yes, I did! After my son died." The guard let go of his legs as Darnex fell into sobs and screams. He gave me no names at all, and simply would not stop screaming. It was a pitiful sight.

As the two guards removed him from his shackles and hoisted him upright, his head lolling with exhaustion, they unthinkingly placed him on his feet. I stepped forward to stop them, but I was a moment too late. As his weeping flesh touched the floor, his screams erupted again and, when they picked him up, pieces of flesh were left as slimy red footprints. All three of us winced, as if a small part of each of our souls suffered with him.

As they placed him back in his cell and re-shackled just one hand, his screams only seemed to get louder. Perhaps he had hoped it would all be over by then. To make matters worse, his wife began screaming too, hurling abuse at everyone she could think of. Her blasphemous language would do nothing to convince me she was not a witch.

The noise was almost unbearable as it echoed through the building. I was within my rights to leave, my work for the day done with one confession, at least, secured. But the man's continued screaming made me uneasy. Had I gone too far? What was wrong with him—surely it was just a little feet heating? I have seen plague victims with wounds rotted to the bone, maggots eating at their bedsores, who complained less than him.

Furthermore, there was a crowd gathered outside for the entertainment, for the horror. And, if I waited until sundown, I could perhaps avoid having to face them.

"I think he may need a barber-surgeon. Perhaps he has been injured..." I said to one of the guards.

He chuckled. "Um, he has been injured. Ain't no barber-surgeons in Satigny. There was one, but he was called up to Geneva in the last plague and never made it back. You couldn't get me near that plague hospital if you paid me a thousand florins. That's the Devil's work. Give me torturing prisoners any day."

"You'd want to be asking Mistress Louise," said the other guard.

"Mistress Louise... You mean Louise de Peney, the... the wisewoman?"

"Aye, if anyone knows, she'll know what to do."

"Can we send for her?"

"If you have a coin, sir, I can ask one of the kids outside."

Donzel, who had been watching with barely concealed amusement throughout the sorry process, was conspicuous in his absence. It was a potentially disastrous situation, since even the *Malleus* is clear a prisoner must under no circumstances die during torture. I thought I had chosen a reasonably safe method.

While waiting for her to arrive, I didn't know what to do with myself. My heart was beating faster, and I was sweating. The noise inside was unbearable, but to go outside was to face the villagers who had been drawn there by the noise. From what I could see through the grille, it appeared that half the *mandement* had congregated. My anxiety was also partly due to the anguish of it all; my whole life, I hadn't so much as raised my voice to another person until I committed that act of shocking violence. And how easy it had been.

But it was also partly the thought that I would finally meet the mysterious woman from the forest. I had felt, from that very first moment, that we had a connection—and perhaps that was it. She would assist me in my task. I thought of Darnex's wife comforting him in his anguish. Someone's arms to fall into... I had a flashback to a moment in my childhood when I had run home crying with a bloodied knee, and my mother had held me tight until I was calm. What would she think if she knew what I had just done? Perhaps it is a relief that she is gone.

In limbo, I paced the corridor. I was growing accustomed to the smell. How anything can become normal. Foulness becomes normal, loneliness becomes normal, and evil becomes normal. When I felt I could stand the wait no longer, I looked through the doorway, and there she was—a slight figure half-running, half-walking along the track, hand in hand with the boy sent to fetch her, with a vast pink sky behind them. The wind had picked up, her cloak flowing behind her, and she had to hold on to her white cap, from which strands of hair blew in all directions. Her movement was urgent, purposeful, and graceful, and I already had a feeling of safety.

"Here she is, sir. Mistress Louise."

She stopped and bowed to me but barely met my eyes, so anxious was she to go inside. "Show me, please," she said and, without waiting, headed into the building.

I followed.

"What happened?" She knelt down next to Darnex, who was still screaming. She felt his brow and took out a piece of cloth to pat it gently.

I began to speak, but only an ugly sound emerged, and I had to clear my throat. "His feet were roasted as part of his questioning."

"And did you do this, sir?" Her tone was accusatory, and my heart sank. Was she disappointed? Perhaps she, too, had thought of me since our strange meeting in the forest.

"I... You are not here to question a city magistrate, mistress. This man is accused of witchcraft."

She swallowed as if trying to contain herself and continued to examine him, feeling his pulse, laying her ear on his chest, and peering at his feet as she held a candle close to them. What little light entered the cell was fading. She did not seem to mind crouching on the filthy floor, touching a man who was festering in his own blood and excrement. She was not afraid of me, and I felt...affronted and thrilled at the same time. She made soothing noises, and the man's cries faded somewhat.

I felt I should say something. "We chose the kindest method we could—"

She looked around sharply. "Kind? Tell me, what is kind here? Because I do not see it."

I was silent again for a few moments. "What is wrong with him?"

"He has a high fever. I must get it down, and then I will treat the burns as best I can." She stood. "I must get supplies from my house."

"I will go. I have a horse."

"No."

"Then I will accompany you." I didn't want to be left alone with that man; I wanted to get away from what I had done, and, most of all, I wanted to feel useful.

"No, sir, if you please. I will go alone." And, as if reading my mind, she said, "If you want to be useful, fetch some water and a cloth and keep him cool. I will be back as soon as I can."

"You may borrow my horse if you like... If you know how to ride, that is..."

"I do. Although it has been a long time, I do. Thank you."

❧

When she returned, as when I had first seen her in the forest, she had two baskets. One was filled with plants and vials of various sorts; the other was covered with a cloth, and I thought I could see its contents moving. There were tiny ripples in the cloth, like a gentle wave on a lake. I thought it was the dim light deceiving me, but when she removed the cloth, the basket was filled with live snails. I recoiled at the sight of their tentacles and muscular contractions as they glided over each other. There had been so many mild horrors this afternoon that I barely raised my eyebrows when I saw her selecting them, preparing to place their flesh onto the soles of his feet.

"Snails? What sorcery is this?"

"Sorcery? You may torture me for this another day, but now I need to cure his burns. The snail jelly will remove the heat and soothe the damaged flesh."

He screamed when she placed the snails on his feet, but he was too exhausted to make much effort to move.

She wrapped them in a tight little hammock of cloth around each foot so their fleshy parts were fashioned to his. They squirmed within the cloth, and it reminded me of maggots, except the creatures were healing, not devouring.

Useless, I went outside. It was pitch dark, and all the villagers had gone home. I inhaled the cold air and shivered, my sweat turning to chill.

After a while, she emerged and sat next to me on the stone bench.

I looked at the ground. "Thank you."

Reading my mind again, she said, "I know you were only trying to do your job. You seem like a good man. They should not have abandoned you to that task."

Those words were like medicine. Warmth flooded me. I felt light-headed, and she must have seen me waver slightly.

"Are you alright?"

"Just a little dizzy."

"You are in shock."

"I suppose you have a cure for that as well."

She smiled. "Perhaps I do. In fact—borage oil would do very well. But I think you will be fine with some rest. And some thought and reflection."

The sky was perfectly clear that night, with a full moon and a whole heaven of stars. I traced them with my eyes. We sat in silence for a long time. I wanted to say everything and nothing.

But eventually, she spoke first, as if to herself. "On nights like this, I always look at those shapes and shadows on the moon and wonder what is there. Mountains, perhaps. I wonder if they are higher than the mountains here. Or, sometimes, I look for a shooting star. On occasion, you can see them, especially at this time of year, I find."

"Once, when I was a child, I saw a long-tailed star..."

"I did too!" She turned to me and smiled.

I did not tell her I knew that she had been a Poor Clare, but I imagined we had been looking out of windows not one hundred feet apart at the very same time.

I was about to ask her what she thought the star meant, but then she said, "It was a comet."

"A comet? Is that some sort of portent?"

"Well, I suppose you could say that. A comet is... Have you read Copernicus?"

"No, I can't say I have. What is it?"

"Copernicus is an astronomer. He wrote a book, just two years past, called On the Revolutions of the Heavenly Spheres. I understand it has been very controversially received. But I heard of it from passing travelers. Whether it is true, I cannot say. Copernicus dared to say that the Earth is continually in motion and therefore cannot be the center of creation."

"The Earth is not the center of God's universe? But that is blasphemy, surely? Heresy."

"I think not." She didn't seem afraid of the accusation. "I think there is something beautifully godly about it, actually. Especially for the reformed faith."

"How so?"

"Well, it diminishes us. It reduces humankind—we are not the center of God's creation. We may even be an afterthought; there may be much more about there. It humbles us. And surely that is what Calvin wants? Who are we to question the mind of God?"

I did not know what to say. It was unthinkable that we might not be the center of the universe. It filled me with unease—with sadness, even. So many people were dying for their beliefs, for the nuances of beliefs, the semantics of faith that becomes everything. We looked up at the stars.

Then I noticed something stirring in the hedgerow opposite us. Something more than a fox. It was a child. Two children. They clambered out and stood holding hands, shivering slightly in the evening chill, wide eyes glinting in the moonlight.

"Oh dear," said Louise. "The Darnex children. They have no other family to take them in tonight. I don't know what to tell them."

She looked at me, and I realized she was expecting me to find a solution and, after all, perhaps it was my responsibility. But what did I know about children? I had been living alone as an adult since the age of twelve.

I stood, beckoning them. "Children, come here. Don't be afraid. Your parents have to stay here tonight."

"Can we stay with them, sir? Can we go in and see them?"

In theory, I could have let them in, but I couldn't bear to let them see their parents like that. For that would truly mean facing what I had done. "No, I'm sorry. The prison is no place for children. Do not worry. Here." I took out my purse and held out a few coins. "Go to the inn, tell Madame Rolette I sent you and that she should give you a meal and a room for tonight."

They stared at the coins in my open hand for a moment, then the boy grabbed them, and they ran away.

"Thank you," said Louise. "That was kind."

For a moment, I beamed with pride that she had seen evidence of my compassion. Then I wondered how much irony there was in her words, in her tone, since a few coins hardly compensated for my torturing their parents.

"You should go and rest, sir. I will stay and watch him through the night."

"No, I will stay."

"Monsieur, I must insist upon it. I need very little sleep, and there is no sense in you exhausting yourself when there is nothing you can do."

I was so tired and filled with relief at the thought of escaping that little piece of Hell I had created, that I agreed. I got up, and she walked over to my horse with me.

"We have had two strange meetings now," she said as I mounted.

"I am afraid I haven't made the best impression."

"No. You haven't. But..." She stopped and wrapped her cloak more tightly around herself against the evening air. She was about to turn back to the prison when she spun around and ventured: "This is a sorry mission, sir. Forgive me if I say that it is beneath you. I can see that it does not become you. If I were you, I would ride back to Geneva and ask to be taken off this case. These villages have had enough. How many witches can there be? It is a sorry business, and it will destroy you. There can be no happy ending to this, whatever the truth. Have you ever seen a burning? Is it not the most terrible thing a person can witness?"

Terrible and irresistible, and... God forgive these thoughts. "It is indeed the sight of a soul entering through the gates of Hell."

"But whose soul? There are other ways to lose your soul."

What could she mean by that? I resolved to think on it when I am alone and not so exhausted.

"Thank you for... well, thank you for everything."

I mounted my horse and by the time I arrived at the inn, I was almost asleep in the saddle. I write this in haste and hope that tonight, exhaustion will render me oblivious to any of the nightly activities that might otherwise disturb my sleep.

❧ 5 ❧

SECRETA MULIERUM

SEPTEMBER 9, 1545

I overslept. When I awoke in the morning, the room was bathed in muted sunlight through the grubby window. As I squinted and rubbed my eyes, there was a sweet moment of blankness before I remembered that I had tortured a man the day before, that the mess I had left was waiting for me and might even be worse. There was a knock on the door. It was Pernette with a bucket of warm water for me to wash myself. That was a luxury indeed, and I allowed her into the room to place it next to the basin, the muscles of her strong arms flexing. She lingered in the room, and I wondered at first if she meant to stay and watch me wash, but she was motioning to something behind me. "Sir, I will empty your chamber pot."

"Ah, no, I will do it," I said, moving towards it, but she resisted, standing in my way coquettishly. "Then let me at least... cover it," I said, mortified, and we both went for the chamber pot at the same time so that the yellow liquid sloshed up against both our hands. I relinquished the pot to her, and she smirked as she bowed her head so her face moved close to the liquid. I did not know what the game was, but I hated it. Who would have servants? Who would have any human interactions at all?

Madame Rolette served me another fine breakfast, but she was less amicable than the previous day. She did question me about the prison-ers, but she already seemed to know the answers, and I sensed an element of hostility. Well, I am not in this village to make friends.

I set off for the prison, approaching with a sense of trepidation and a heavy feeling of responsibility. I desperately wanted to never go back into that miserable dungeon.

When I reached the door, all was quiet. No sign of the two chil-dren, although a few peasants dawdled, whispering to each other on their way to the fields. The guard at the door, who had been dozing in the morning sunshine, woke with a jolt as I thumped on the heavy wooden door, as careful as always not to touch the handle.

"Morning, Magistrate. Here, I'll let you in."

"Any news?"

"No, all quiet; a peaceful night. Mistress Louise stayed up for most of it, cleaning the place up."

I went in to examine the misery I had created. The stench was still in the dungeon, but I could also smell herbs and lemon. Both prisoners were asleep, but the man stirred as a shaft of light from the grille hit him directly in the face, and he turned his head from side to side to try to escape it. He was lying propped up on clean straw and blankets that someone must have procured during the night.

Louise was asleep in a seated position against the corner wall. She had taken no straw or blankets for herself. I watched her for a few moments—the rise and fall of her breast, the fluttering of her eyelids, the stray fair hairs tumbling around her face and neck. She was exhausted and disheveled and beautiful, and I was struck by the urge to draw closer, kneel in front of her, and tuck that hair back into the cap.

"Pretty, ain't she?" said a feeble, gravelly voice from behind me. Darnex was awake and eyeing me wearily.

I was chagrined that he had seen me looking at her.

"She saved my life last night," he said. "She's like an angel. A spirit."

"Monsieur Darnex. Do you stand by what you said yesterday? That you renounced God and gave yourself to the Devil?"

He recoiled from me and shuddered.

I heard a voice from behind me again. Disturbed by our voices, Louise had woken up.

"Monsieur Darnex cannot take any more of your tortures. I absolutely forbid it."

"You absolutely forbid nothing, Mademoiselle."

But Monsieur Darnex put up his hand. "It's alright; I stand by it. But I don't know about nobody else. What will happen now?"

"Now, I will interview your wife. Mademoiselle de Peney, since the *châtelain* has not yet arrived, will you be our witness?"

"I will not. I am already embroiled far more than I wish to be in this sordid business. I will go home to rest." Louise had risen to her feet, smoothing down her skirts and collecting her things. I realized she was preparing to leave, and a sudden panic struck me; I did not want to be left alone with the prisoners, but most of all, I wanted so very much for her to stay.

She leaned over Monsieur Darnex, felt his brow, and whispered some comforting words to him; how I wished she would do the same to me! When she stood up, she looked at me for a long time. I knew the look was meaningful, and perhaps I was supposed to understand the meaning, but I did not; perhaps I was supposed to say something, but I did not. Eventually, she shook her head and took her leave, and I felt as much a prisoner as the sorry Darnex pair, left in the fetid darkness to ponder the mysteries of women. What had she meant when she looked into my eyes? Disappointment, surely, but if she was disappointed in me, then it means she sees me as capable of finer things. And impertinence, too, for a woman to stare so defiantly at a man in authority. Indeed, nobody has ever looked at me so intently—it was hypnotic, bewitching even.

My heart was still racing when Donzel finally arrived. Under his irritating gaze, I interviewed Madame Darnex, who—in contrast to the previous day—was calm and collected.

"Madame Darnex, what say you to the charges that the Folliez baby died at your hands by your witchcraft?"

"I don't know nothing about no witchcraft. But I loved that baby. I am grieving for that baby as I grieved for my own. I wanted nothing but the best for him. If only I had..."

"What?"

"I should've... I should've done more. Madame Folliez had no milk, you see. She wanted a wet nurse, to be like those fancy women in the city. She liked the idea of it, to be the fancy gentlewoman, you know. But you can't have it both ways; you can't take your baby back after a few weeks and expect to feed it yerself. She had no milk. And I knew that. But I couldn't stop her. She was so filled with melancholy and jealousy, and she wanted her baby back, wanted me out of the house. I brought a special tea for her to drink to help with her milk. But I don't know if she drank it. And I should have done more; it wasn't enough. Maybe I should've tried to feed the baby in secret. Maybe I should've..."

Whatever had happened, she evidently blamed herself.

"This special tea you speak of. Where did you get it?"

She paused before answering. "It was from my garden. Just herbs—it's what women do. What'll happen now? What'll happen to my husband?"

"He has renounced God. He will most probably be banished. That is what I will recommend. He must go to Geneva for trial—we do not have the proper facilities here."

She was shaking her head and crying.

"The penalty could be worse, you know," I said. "For heresy. He has admitted heresy."

"Stupid idiot of a husband. He's a God-fearing man—I swear to you on my life, on my own child's grave. He's talking rubbish. He would have said anything not to get me into trouble. Banished? Then he'll die. He can't even walk now. And even if he could—he doesn't know how to look after hisself. What do I have to do to be banished with him? I suppose that's the best fate we can hope for?"

I thought for a moment. Two banishments and case closed—that is not what Calvin sent me to do. I was not convinced the sorry couple had anything whatsoever to do with witchcraft. But if I could at least get another name, then I could take this further. Find the true evil in this village. "Madame Darnex, if you can give me names—even one person—it will certainly help your case."

She paused for a long time, then her eyes lit up. "Blaise Besson."

"Blaise Besson? Who is she?"

"The prostitute, Blaise. She was the one, yes! She was the one who gave me the…the special tea."

"But I thought it was from your garden?"

"No, it was definitely from her. She has potions, you know, for helping men with their members, and she said this would help Madame Folliez with her breasts. I should never have believed her. And you know…" She was becoming more animated, more convinced. "There are so many rumors about her. She is a terrible woman—they say she steals men's members, that she goes to the Sabbath, that she…" Her voice dropped to a whisper. "…that she copulates with devils."

"Why did you not tell me this before?"

"I…was afraid. I was not sure. But now, I am sure. And you'll help with our case? So, we can avoid banishment?"

Around midday, Monsieur Darnex's fever went up, as Louise had said it would, and I rode to her house to get more medicine. What a pleasure to conduct the day's errands in such fresh air. And I cannot deny I was intrigued to see her again, away from the horrors of the prison, and to see where and how she lived. The guards had told me where to find her house, which was set apart from but within easy distance of all the other villages in the *mandement*. The guards' directions took me back along the Nant d'Avril and into the Satigny forest, where I had first seen her. How things had changed—how I had changed—in only two days. I was already looking forward to the evening when I could be alone with my thoughts of her. Indeed, I already struggle to remember what I used to think about before her.

As the trees began to thin and clear, I saw a building. Three red squirrels darting up a tree just in front of me seemed to confirm that it was hers.

I should not have been surprised by the size and beauty of her house since it was the seat of the de Peney family. Her relatives had owned land in the area for centuries. Yet I was still taken aback, for the idea of a woman living alone in that place was unthinkable. How had she protected it? How did she protect herself? The house was in the middle of its own field, and although it was well-protected by the forest, the surrounding low stone wall left it completely open to view. Perhaps two hundred years old, the house had walls made of similar sturdy, rough stone, with a roof showing signs of deterioration. The front garden had been allowed to grow over on either side of the path in a rather pleasant fashion, like a meadow of long grass dotted with flowers. A lone goat was tied in the middle of the grass by a long rope. Upon my arrival, the creature stopped its methodical eating to eye me suspiciously. It was a huge animal, almost the size of a cow, with a bell dangling around its neck and ripe, pendulous udders.

I found myself instinctively veering to the far side of the path to edge past the animal, which continued to watch me. As always, I was drawn to the door knocker, a plain iron ring that I had no intention of touching. I thumped on the wooden door with my fist, but there was no answer. I had a sense that she was there, however, and then realized I could hear a female voice singing from somewhere beyond the house. I walked around the side to the back garden, which bore an impressive array of ordered plant beds, one of which rustled with activity. Louise was facing away from me, crouched amongst the plants, where her arms were moving busily, weeding or harvesting. I couldn't tell. Her voice was light and full of enthusiasm as she sang a song I didn't recognize.

Au joli bois en l'ombre d'un souci,
M'y faut aller pour passer ma tristesse.
Rempli de deuil d'un souvenir transi,
Manger m'y faut maintes poires d'angoisse.
En un jardin rempli de noires fleurs,
De mes deux yeux ferai larmes et pleurs.
Fi de liesse et hardiesse! Regret m'oppresse
Puisque j'ai perdu mes amours.
Las trop j'endure. Le temps m'y dure. Je vous assure:
Soulas vous n'avez plus de cours.

. . .

It was a ballad about spending time in a pretty forest to assuage the loss of love. A sad song in a minor key, yet it was a wistful, rather than desperate sadness. Her voice filled me with both joy and melancholy as if it was the song I had been waiting to hear my whole life. The simple melody invited itself to be harmonized by multiple voices, like the glorious chants Calvin is creating for our people, and I was almost tempted to join in as I do in church. I had a few moments to observe her unnoticed before she got to the end of her song, sat back on her haunches to mop her brow, and caught sight of me.

She stood, and I noticed she was in no hurry to roll down her sleeves or her skirt before finally curtseying. *"Monsieur le magistrat."*

"Mademoiselle Louise. That is a beautiful song. I don't believe I have heard it before." I called her by her first name; what a thrill to hear the word said out loud and by my voice!

"No? It is *'Joli bois'* by Claude de Sermisy. He is a composer at the court of the French king. Our French refugees have brought us many songs, and since I left the cloister—I was a Poor Clare, as I expect you have been told—I often allow myself the indulgence of singing something that is not a hymn. That is not a crime, is it?"

It was not, but I didn't know how to answer. "I...I thought perhaps you might be sleeping."

"Oh no, there is too much to do. And I need little sleep. Years of training." She smiled, and I must have looked blank. "At the convent. We were woken every four hours for prayer. And I attend many births. Babies come at all hours and often at night."

"Ah. What a beautiful day."

She looked dismayed for some reason. "Perhaps for us. Not so for the prisoners."

I cursed myself for my misplaced observation. Why can I not say the simplest greeting without getting it wrong?

"How is Monsieur Darnex?" she asked.

"He is quiet, but his fever has been up again since midday. That's why I am here—to collect some more of those herbs you gave him."

"Of course. I will show you how to administer them, and you may do it yourself. And his wife? What did you do with her?"

I winced at the insinuation in her tone. "I questioned her only, mademoiselle. She appears very guilty."

"She may indeed feel deep regret for what happened, but that does not make her guilty. A baby she loved died not long after her own baby died. And, now that she is in prison, she cannot take care of her own children. Mothers are ruled by guilt at the best of times. So, what else would you expect? With respect, sir."

Again, that fearless chastisement of a city magistrate. I had no answer, and we were squinting at each other in the bright sunlight.

She dusted her hands on her apron and looked about her with a slight impatience. "Can I offer you a glass of ale, monsieur? I certainly need one myself; this is thirsty work."

"Yes, thank you,"

She led the way through the garden to the back of the house as I admired the plentiful beds of vegetables and herbs. There was a little orchard brimming with ripe apples, a set of wooden beehives, and chickens and geese wandering about. Within the city walls, there is no greenery like that, and I would have had no idea how to grow anything. After my parents died, I ate only at school, supplemented by whatever I could steal from market stalls. I went to bed each night, filled with either hunger or shame.

I had to stoop to pass through the kitchen doorway, but once inside, it was light and spacious. It felt more like an apothecary shop than a kitchen, though—so filled with jars, bottles, and hanging bunches of dried plants. Something was steaming in a large black cauldron hung over the fire, and on the table was an array of glassware linked by earthen piping that appeared to be in the middle of a complex distillation. It smelled of lemons, basil, and lavender, heady and delightful.

"Please, go into the parlor, and I will bring your drink," she said, directing me through to the front of the house.

I went into a room larger than any you would find in the city. There were shelves filled with books, and I fingered them, imagining myself as the man of the house—where I would put my desk and my own treasured book collection. The furniture was faded, worn, and thread-bare but bore the hallmarks of aristocratic family history.

I was drawn to a magnificent oak chest, intricately carved with all manner of things—a village scene with tiny people, a Virgin Mary, and a Christ figure, each panel decorated with leaf and star patterns. I traced some of them slowly with my finger, suddenly not afraid to touch unknown things. The workmanship was extraordinary.

I was shaken from my reverie when I realized she was standing behind me, holding a glass of ale. "This is a fine house," I said. "Do you live here alone?"

She nodded. "Since my sister and her husband died. I know it does not belong to me, that it should pass into the male line, but everyone I know has died. And, as you can imagine, I have not been keen to search out long-lost relatives. No doubt someone will take it from me eventually, but until then, I shall... Well, I have nowhere else."

"It is a precarious existence. A woman should not live alone."

"I have found a place, a use for myself here. And I like to live alone."

"Did you never think to marry? You must have had suitors."

"I am nearly thirty years old, sir. Not such a great prospect, despite my house. And, as I said, I like to live alone."

"As do I. My family is also dead. Plague, of course."

"I am sorry. And what about you, sir? Did you never think to marry?"

"I also like to be alone."

"It comes to something when the priests and nuns of this world are marrying, and it is the lawyers and magistrates who are chaste."

There was a pause while I tried to think of something to say, aware that it should fall to me to direct proceedings. "No servants here?"

"Servants? And how would I afford that, sir? I am a servant myself."

"A servant yourself?"

"I serve the people of these villages. They pay me when they can, and I have almost everything I need."

There was another pause, and I filled it by walking back over to her bookshelves and perusing them. It was a fine collection, mostly reli-gious texts, but with many works by Greek philosophers and mathematicians. I wondered whether Louise owned any forbidden books; I wondered if she too sought out the books that had temptations and perversions hidden in the margins. I imagine she does. I saw one new-looking volume, The Great Book of Surgery, titled in German.

"You have read Paracelsus?" I asked.

"Not only have I read him, I have met him. He visited our convent in 1530 and stayed for several weeks. He is a great man and taught me many things even in that short time. Most of the books you see here belonged to my family, but the volume of Paracelsus is mine—it was the only book I could carry when we left the convent. Apart from my Bible, of course."

"He is an alchemist, I have heard?"

She smiled. "You say the word alchemist with a tone of suspicion, and you are not the only one. Paracelsus was hounded from Germany by those who accused him of dark arts. But he was a brilliant doctor, a brilliant scientist. He even had an idea for how to prevent the spread of plague by administering minuscule doses to healthy citizens. He called it inoculation."

"Then he was a plague-spreader?"

"Quite the opposite, sir. In any case, his idea was far too controversial to be attempted and remains a theory only. Most importantly for me, Paracelsus is not afraid of the mysteries of the female body." She smiled at my blush and continued. "You know, the convent was a veritable lying-in hospital. Women came from all over Geneva to give birth, and he improved our practices no end."

"He was present at births? That is beyond inappropriate."

She laughed but kindly. "So shocked, sir! When we are told that real medicine is the work of men."

"But surely childbirth is women's work?"

"Do you know what the great Luther said about childbirth? He said, 'If women die in childbed, that does no harm. It is what they were made for.' Paracelsus believes we are worth more than that. Anyway." She had been holding the book and looked as if she was about to show me a page, but then she abruptly changed her mind and put it back on the shelf as if to close the conversation.

I had an urge to stay, to talk to her, to be in that house, to avoid the prison. But I could sense an agitation that her politeness masked.

Eventually, she got up, saying, "Let me fetch you those herbs. He will need to be treated soon."

She went to the kitchen and returned with a leather pouch from which she tipped four black pills to show me. "This is called laudanum. Indeed, it was Paracelsus who showed me how to prepare it. Made from the seeds of poppies that he brought from the Orient, mixed with a little lemon juice, and dried in dung with a tiny amount of gold. Monsieur Darnex should swallow two of them with some ale—keep the other two for tomorrow."

"You cannot come to treat him yourself?"

"I will try to come tonight, but I promised to visit a new mother in Peissy first."

"You are in demand."

She nodded, standing quite still, her hands clasped politely in front of her, and I felt myself being edged toward the front door.

"A nun must serve," she said. "I mean...I am no longer a nun, of course, but I believe the best way to serve God is to serve thy neighbor. Incurvature in se. A life lived inwards is no life at all."

I did not respond. I felt a dull ache that I could not pinpoint.

So, she continued, kindly filling the silence. "Have you not heard Pastor Bernard yet? This is his favorite subject, incurvature in se."

"Mademoiselle Louise, do you think the lying-in maid is guilty? Do you think the mother could be mistaken?"

She sighed and softened her stance. "Women are like animals around the time of birth. They inhabit what is most true about human nature."

"You mean they succumb to their baser instincts?"

"No, their finer instincts. It is very powerful to be around them at this time. It is a profound, inspiring thing. But women are also very vulnerable at this stage. There is a lot of jealousy. And many times, I have seen a profound melancholy set in after a few weeks, especially amongst wealthier women who have employed lying-in maids. It interferes with the bond between mother and child. It is a sacred bond. And when there is sacred, there is also..." She trailed off and asked, "What will happen to the prisoners?"

"It is a good outcome for them, I think. They will escape with banishment."

"You consider banishment a good outcome, sir? How will they survive while he cannot walk? Where will they go—Savoy? They will be tried as heretics twice over."

"He renounced God, mademoiselle. That is the ultimate form of heresy."

"Under duress. That is absurd. Wouldn't you feel like renouncing God? If your child had died? And his wife has not admitted any guilt, has she?"

"Ah, on the contrary. She has admitted knowledge of a plot. And she has given me a name. She says that Blaise Besson cursed the baby. She says that Besson is a witch."

We were on the doorstep by then, and Louise looked exasperated at the mention of Besson.

"Blaise is a prostitute of a certain age. She has lain with every man in this village, including Monsieur Darnex. If Susanne had to name someone, it would be her. I know you are trying to create Calvin's godly society. I know you believe that. But this is not the way. The Devil is here, yes. But not in these women. The Devil is in all of our souls. Including mine. Including yours."

I was indignant that she should presume to know my soul but at the same time, a little thrilled. Does the Devil come to tempt her the same way he tempts me? Perhaps she means that we have the same desires. But I had no answer for her, and I backed down the path a little. "Mademoiselle, thank you for these herbs. I trust I will see you later."

I turned and cried out, having almost walked into that infernal goat that had wandered into the middle of the pathway, still staring at me. I hoped Louise had closed the door and not witnessed my humiliation, but then she called to me, and I was forced to turn around.

"Monsieur le magistrate. If I may, I would advise that you do not lie with Blaise. She will offer. Well, I suppose you may do whatever you wish with your prisoners..."

"How dare you accuse me of such a thing? What do you take me for? I am a city magistrate and a godly man. Prostitution is a sin. Lying with a woman outside of marriage is a sin. Lying with a prisoner is a sin. All these things are punishable by death." I swelled with pleasure as I saw her superior position finally deflate.

"I apologize. It's just... She is riddled with syphilis, sir. Quite mad with it, in fact. I just wanted to warn you. Since you are innocent of what goes on around here."

"Thank you, mademoiselle. I am indeed innocent. And you have nothing to fear."

I swung myself onto my horse, buoyed by my new moral high ground. It was where I much preferred to be. Where there is sacred, there is also profane. How right she was. She must read the same books as me, read the same texts, and think the same thoughts. And if women are as insatiable as I am told... But she also mentioned my innocence of what goes on around here. There is clearly much to investigate in this village.

❧

Having guards at my disposal is certainly a novelty. I never had anyone at my disposal before. After giving Darnex his medicine, I informed him and his wife that they would be transferred to the city for sentencing and that banishment was the most likely outcome. I also allowed their children to visit. I enjoyed this healing, soothing aspect. It was far more powerful than the powers I had so far been using. But I must remember I am here to administer justice. And sometimes God is cruel as well as He is merciful.

I then instructed two guards to accompany me to arrest Blaise Besson, although I realized I did not know where she lived.

The guards chuckled. "Everyone knows where she lives, Magistrate. Follow us."

I had hoped not to make any more of a spectacle of myself than I already had, but I suppose that was too much to ask. It was late afternoon, and people were returning from the fields, so there were clusters in the square, with straggling groups following me and the guards. What an awkward and unpleasant procession we made.

By the time we arrived at Besson's house, there was quite a crowd. I could sense a certain glee amidst the hushed chatter, which was soon confirmed. I thumped on the door, avoiding the knocker as usual, but there was no answer. I waited for a moment, with the crowd hushed, then I stepped forward and knocked again.

"Madame Blaise Besson," I called in the loudest voice I had ever used. "Open up in the name of the law."

There was still nothing, and the guards obviously thought me too timid because one stepped forward. "Stand aside, if you please, magistrate."

He slammed on the door with the pike of his halberd and yelled the same words as I had but with at least twice the volume. There was a clattering inside the house, a thudding of feet downstairs, and the three of us stepped back as the door opened and a sheepish-looking man crept out, still buttoning his doublet. The crowd erupted with laughter, and I reddened as much as the man, who darted away down a side alley, closely followed by a woman screaming threats and obscenities at him—whom I could only assume was his wife.

It was supposed to be a solemn legal process but had turned into a farce, a ribald entertainment.

Then in the doorway stood Blaise herself. I recognized her instantly as the woman who had been in the pillory the day I arrived. She had perhaps been attractive once, but the ravages of age, poverty, and disease had not been kind, and she probably looked far older than her years.

She looked haggard and disheveled; her skirts were hitched around her legs, and her bustier was half undone. A cap had been hastily placed on her head, but graying-blonde hair fell in straggles about her face. Her stockings had been pulled up, but she wore no shoes. The skin rashes, and lesions were evident around her ankles. How any man could bring himself to lie with her, I could not understand. She would have been arrested within minutes had she set foot in Geneva's walls. Calvin was right; there is work to be done on social morality here.

She draped herself in the doorway and took in the crowd open-mouthed yet languid, defiant, squinting into the square—I have heard that one of the symptoms of syphilis was gradual blindness—and there was a silence as if she was about to perform. Her eyes suddenly came to life, and she burst into raucous laughter, doubling over and slapping her legs. Then she stopped just as quickly as she had started, leaning against the doorway again. I could see that she was drunk.

"What's this then?" she squawked.

I cleared my throat and repeated, "Madame Blaise Besson, you are to be arrested following an accusation of witchcraft."

"You jest, sir. I never done any witchcraft in my life."

"Madame, you will be held at the prison for questioning. You can either walk with us in a genteel manner..."

At this, I was interrupted by snorts of "Genteel?" from the crowd and then by Blaise herself.

"I ain't going to no prison! I ain't no witch! No woman accused of sorcery ever comes out!" As the guards grabbed her, she hurled expletives and sexual references that made me both prick up my ears and want to cover them—things even worse than those described in the *Malleus Maleficarum*.

The guards had taken over then, and a tipcart and ropes had been brought from somewhere, directed, it appeared, by Donzel. Yet again, proceedings had taken on a life of their own. I must remember that this is all God's will.

As they tied the ropes, her skirts hitched up on the tipcart, so I saw the sores further up her legs and the beginnings of dark hair in her crevices. The guards hoisted the handles to wheel her off, tipping her upright enough that she could look at the crowd as we left.

Eyes wild, she raged. "All of you should be on your guard now! None of you are safe! The things I know!" Then she laughed again. "It doesn't matter what I know! I can say whatever I like! Who should I take down with me?"

I knew that she was right. According to the *Malleus*, all forms of witness testimony must be considered by the investigator. And the villagers seemed to know it too because a hush had fallen over the crowd, and the laughter had stopped as they sloped away.

As I mounted my horse to follow the cart back to the prison, I saw Bernard motionless next to the fountain, oblivious to the people moving by him, looking at me with an expression I could not decipher.

So, there was a third prisoner, and I was faced with the problem of where to put her since I only had two cells. I shuddered at the noise there would be if I put her in the same one as her accuser, so I had Susanne Darnex moved into her husband's cell, leaving Blaise with a cell to herself. We gave her some ale and bread and left her to stew for a time while I composed myself.

A small part of me wanted to try the torture methods again to see if I could get it right. And, if I didn't, who would care? About a half-mad, half-dead whore? She was a veritable experimentation table.

Indeed, Donzel, who was loitering outside the prison, said, "You can throw caution to the wind with this one, Magistrate! I envy you—if you need any help, you know where I am!"

"What in God's name do you mean?"

"For example, she will need to be pricked."

"As you well know, Donzel, the witch-pricking and shaving must be done by a certified barber-surgeon, which you do not have here."

"And torture must be done by a certified executioner, but that didn't stop you yesterday, did it, man?" He clapped me on the back, guffawing, but he was right.

I was swimming no less out of my depth than I had been the day before. But I needn't have worried because Blaise gave me everything and more.

"Madame, you are accused of the grievous crime of witchcraft, that you did procure a potion that poisoned the mother's milk of Madame Folliez and killed her baby. What say you to these charges?"

Before I finished recounting the official accusation, she interrupted, "I will tell you. I don't know nothing about no mother's milk potion. But I know about potions, that I do. Men come to me, and sometimes they are old or infirm or shy, and their manhood does not do what it should. Well, if they cannot get their pleasure, they do not pay me. And so, why would I not help them out with a special remedy? What harm does a little magic do?"

"Magic is heresy, Madame. All forms of sorcery come from the Devil. Where did you get this remedy?"

Her eyes sparkled. "From the Devil, as you say. Yes, the Devil came to me in the night, and he whispered that if I pledged allegiance to him, he could help me with my business."

"What did he look like, this Devil? Was he in human or animal form?"

"Oh, he was in human form, sir. He was fat, with a pointy beard and brightly colored clothes, and he roared with laughter. And he smelled of strong liquor and shit and piss, oh yes. But he had a huge, long stick, and I rode it all night, yes, I did." She doubled over in crazed laughter, and I had to wait for her to compose herself.

"Madame, are you saying that you took aerial flight with the Devil?"

She burst into laughter again. "I suppose that is what I am saying. I rode on his huge long stick all night, I did."

"Did it fly through the air?"

"In a manner of speaking, yes. I have heard it said, and so I shouted, 'White stick, black stick, carry me where you will go. Go, in the Devil's name, go!'"

"And did you attend a Sabbath?"

"Oh yes, I did attend a Sabbath."

"Can you describe what happened at this Sabbath to me?"

She appeared to be almost enjoying the narrative by then, drawing upon theatrical reserves and using wild hand movements to describe the scene to me. "It was a big celebration, hidden in the middle of a thick forest: torches and candles and a big roaring fire. There were lots of people and music and dancing and feasting. And in the middle was the Devil on his throne, and all the women had to pay homage to him by curtseying with their backsides."

"And how did you pledge allegiance to the Devil?"

"Well, I had to kiss him under his tail, you know, like you're supposed to. And oh, it smelled so foul."

"And did you renounce God and Jesus Christ?"

"I...not in so many words, magistrate."

"And what else happened at this Sabbath?"

"There was feasting... There were roasted babies, you know, just as we have all heard. Oh yes, I saw it with my own eyes. And dancing, such dancing. All manner of perversions and sodomy, sir. All made the beast with two backs, but the Devil took the best women for himself."

It was lunatic raving—I knew it—but I was entranced and could not have moved from my position without some discomfort, without revealing my arousal.

"Who was in attendance at this Sabbath? Anyone from this village that you recognized?"

She thought for a moment. "All wore masks, terrible animal masks."

"But you must have recognized someone. If you give me some names, it will help your cause."

"Let me see. Goodwife Drouz was there, you know, the old hag, of course she was. And oh yes, Claudine Rey, the one with the Devil's child. And the Devil's child was there too. And Mistress Jeanne, the plague-worker's wife. She should have burned already with the rest of her family; I said it at the time."

A Devil's child, a plague-worker, I thought. Very likely to be witches. Despite her lunatic raving, Blaise Besson knew so many details about Sabbath activities that it sounded convincing. My heart leaped. With very little effort, I had secured a spontaneous confession, without torture, and a host of names with which to continue my investigation. Calvin would be pleased with my work.

"Don't you want to hear the end of the story then, sir?"

I shook myself back into the room. "Yes, continue. What happened at the end of the Sabbath? How did you get the potion?"

"Well, I fornicated with the Devil, didn't I? And his member was so long and thin, and his semen was cold as ice. It sent a chill into my heart. And this semen was the potion he gave me."

"Why did he give you the potion? Was it to kill unbaptized children?"

"Yes, exactly that. You know what you're about, don't you, Magistrate? And now, would you like to take your pleasure with she who has copulated with the Devil himself?" She lifted her skirt and pulled back hairy purple folds of flesh from around her center, and I looked away and left the room, her laughter echoing around the damp ceiling vaults.

When I returned to the inn, exhausted after the day's upheavals, my heart sank to see Bernard in the square outside, pacing with his hands behind his back. I had a feeling he was there waiting for me, and I was right. So few people in the countryside, yet so little peace. Could I never be alone? At least, I thought it was not Donzel. I truly did not have the energy for him.

But Bernard looked less friendly than usual, and he almost blocked my path to the inn's door. "Well?"

"She has made a spontaneous confession."

"That she killed the child?"

"No, not exactly. But she has…"

"I fear these are the ravings of a madwoman. You cannot take them as any sort of evidence."

"She has named several women of the village as being seen at a witches' Sabbath."

He suddenly looked anxious. "Who did she name?"

Aware of his agitation, I took out my notes and read, "Leonarda Drouz, Claudine and Clauda Rey, and Jeanne Valleron." I looked up in time to see his shoulders drop, and I sensed a slight relief from him. There was an awkward pause, and I wondered which of us was supposed to speak next.

Eventually, Bernard said, motioning to the inn behind him, "I wondered if we might dine together? I'm sure the company here is not what you are used to. And I'd certainly welcome news from the city. At the very least," he offered, smiling, "I could bring you some protection from the relentless Madame Rolette so that you can enjoy your food in peace."

Without a ready excuse, I smiled back, and we headed inside. The truth was I had had more company in the village than in a whole year in the city. There was a part of me that wanted to be alone with my thoughts and the *Malleus*. And another part of me felt that if I started talking for the first time in my life, I might never stop. How much would I reveal?

We sat in the quietest corner of the inn, under the eaves. A fire blazed and crackled in the hearth, and Madame Rolette brought us ale and a meat stew that was undeniably fine. I began to relax. But Bernard was not relaxed, and I knew he was there with an agenda.

"If I may, Magistrate. Blaise Besson is not in full control of her mental faculties. The ravages of syphilis, you know? She would have been listing whatever gossip she could think of. There may be truth in it, there may not. And a certain amount of vindictiveness would be understandable, given her position. Don't forget, only the day you arrived, she was in the pillory, and not for the first time." He took a gulp of ale.

"The first woman—Leonarda Drouz—she and Blaise have been engaged in a terrible quarrel for years. When Leonarda's husband was alive, he was one of Blaise's regular...customers, shall we say. Leonarda was justified in her anger, of course—he was spending what little money they had. She eventually stopped him from going, and that was a large portion of Blaise's income lost. So, Blaise has always had a vendetta against her. And, of course, now Drouz is a widow, little more than a beggar. No one will miss her, sadly—they will thank us for getting rid of her." Roars of laughter erupted from the bar, and a group of farmers launched into a bawdy song accompanied by Madame Rolette.

Bernard smiled tolerantly and waited for their noise to subside before continuing. "And then the poor Rey family, Claudine and Clauda. The daughter has been known in these parts as the Devil's Child since the day she was born. The husband abandoned them, of course. It's a miracle that either of them is still alive." Then he looked worried as if he had incriminated them by accident. Miracle is a dangerous word these days.

He moved on quickly. "And then Jeanne Valleron, you said. They were a family of plague workers living on the outskirts of the mandement in a plague-working community. She is the only one left now. Her husband and sister were burned for plague-spreading just this spring, and the rest of the family succumbed to the disease itself. So, it is no wonder she is still under suspicion."

"How did she ever escape the first investigation?"

"She was pregnant. The baby died, of course."

"As you say, there may be truth in it, there may not. And, in that case, it all warrants investigating."

"Of course. You must do your job. It's just... Aubert, have you read much Erasmus?"

"Of course."

"I have read his letters to Martin Luther. In one, he said, 'I see how much easier it is to start than to assuage a tumult.' Once you have started down this route, it will be very difficult to turn back. And lives, families, are at stake."

I was silent, torn as to how much more to tell him. I looked around, then leaned forward conspiratorially and lowered my voice, not that anyone could have heard us.

"You know, she spoke of terrible things, this prostitute. The Devil, the Sabbath, feasting upon dead children, terrible crimes of fornication. And a potion. She spoke of a potion to, a potion to..." I reddened as I tried to get the words out.

Fortunately, Bernard finished my sentence. "A potion to help restore a man's...manhood."

"You have heard of such things?"

He seemed remarkably relaxed. "I suppose it is part of her job to... and yes, I know, I know." He held up his hands. "Her job is illegal, and she would long have been arrested in the city. But it is not unthinkable that she and her clients might need such a remedy. And if one exists, a simple powder or unguent, for a harmless—"

My fist slammed down a little too hard. "It is not harmless!"

He backtracked immediately. "I'm sorry. I suppose I meant within the boundaries of marriage."

"In any case, a potion like that is white magic, and St. Augustine tells us that all magic is the Devil's work, be it black or white. All magic involves the evocation of a demon—even if its purposes are not harmful—because it is part of the Devil's plan to lure humanity away from God."

At that moment, there was a raucous cackle from the bar.

Bernard looked troubled, and we both knew why. I imagine he wanted to talk about the loss of magic—what had been lost with the loss of the Catholic faith and the danger it posed to those who still believed it, who needed it. But it was too dangerous. I imagine he wanted to talk about Louise. But it was too dangerous. I think we both knew that when we spoke of potions, we were referring to Louise.

Eventually, he could not resist, but his tone was gentle. "In the city, you have hospitals, apothecaries, doctors. Here, we do not. We had a doctor, but he left with a bout of plague three years ago and never returned. What we have here is knowledge passed down from generation to generation. I know we are on the brink of a new science. But sometimes I fear that the barber-surgeons, now they don't have monks' tonsures to attend to, are merely trying to carve out a bigger role for themselves. And Paracelsus, surely the greatest scientist of our time, tells us, 'There is nothing in Heaven and Earth that is not also in man.' The art of healing comes from nature, not from the physician. Therefore, the physician must start from nature, with an open mind."

Somehow, I knew he had gotten that from Louise, and I smarted at it.

I realized I still hadn't spoken. Sometimes, my own thoughts are so powerful and so at the forefront of my mind that I am not sure whether or not they have come out as speech. And then, at other times, I blurt out a thought that I should have kept to myself. Fortunately, Bernard continued.

"I don't know. I am just a priest." He saw me bristle at the word 'priest', and quickly corrected himself. "A pastor, I mean, forgive me. The old words still come out by accident sometimes. But I do sometimes wonder if the only difference between medicine and white magic is that the one is practiced by doctors, and the other by women and healers."

We looked at each other, then away, then looked at each other again. Then tried to feign interest in our food, ale, the rowdy goings-on at the bar, anything. I may not be very well-versed in diagnosing the minutiae of my own feelings, but I know that they were the first stirrings of romantic rivalry. We knew we were both thinking about Louise and why should he not have designs on her? A cleric and a former nun, both young, of marriageable age, of comparably good appearance... Surely, it was only a matter of time before he made a proposal. Indeed, the fact that they are not married puts Bernard in a questionable light. Why had he not already made his move?

Bernard, perhaps thinking along the same lines—*why can I never tell what people are really thinking? Can people tell what I am thinking?* —was eager to change the subject. He brightened, too, to change the mood. "Tell me, what is it like in the city now?"

"When were you last there?"

"All the city pastors are supposed to attend the weekly meetings of the Company of Pastors. But I do not have a horse; it is a day's walk, and I am needed here—so I usually make do with letters. It has been some months now. I do not know the city well at all."

"I don't understand. How have you never lived in the city? Where did you receive your training?"

"In France." He looked at me, a little wary. "I was a priest."

I almost whispered, "You were a Catholic priest?"

"Yes, and I gladly converted after seeing the light! Many of us did. We are the most prized of all the new pastors, you know—the ones who saw the light of the true faith and converted—we are considered as having the most zeal. I am the only one in Geneva, though. I am rather proud of that, I must own. I was specially selected by Calvin himself after we met in Strasbourg. He wanted a reformed Catholic in a place such as this, where not everyone is convinced, to reassure people, to show them that conversion is not only a possible thing but a fine and beautiful thing."

"And it was not difficult for you to renounce your faith?"

"Not at all. I do not see it as renouncing my faith. As I said, I saw the light. The true path of Christ."

Again, we were treading dangerous ground, and he believed I was testing him. But I wasn't; I simply struggled to find a suitable conversation. And I was distracted because all I could think about was the fact that he had even more in common with Louise than I had realized. Both are former Catholics; both had taken vows—celibacy, poverty, chastity—and I can compete with those things practically but not spiritually. If she has retained any of her former ascetic beliefs, she will not be impressed by my city money or manners, and, on the moral battlefield, I had not made the best start to my campaign—from her perspective, at least. But we have this connection, and I am sure she feels it too. I was relieved that my dinner with Bernard was almost at an end.

SERMONES VULGARES

SEPTEMBER 10, 1545

I was unsure how to proceed. Whether they were the ravings of a madwoman or a desperate woman lashing out in hatred and jealousy, Blaise's claims had to be investigated. I decided to spend the next day visiting the accused individually, without guards or the threat of arrest, to see whether I could get a sense of what was really going on.

The next morning, with directions from Bernard, I set out to the house of Leonarda Drouz. I should say dwelling, for only an optimist could have described it as a house. Madame Drouz lives in the ruins of an old stone building, which was perhaps a tiny chapel once, that had been covered with salvaged pieces of wood, tile, clay, and branches and hay added over the top to create some semblance of walls and a roof. It is almost like living outdoors, and I was immediately struck with the thought that an old woman would be better off dying now than facing the freezing snow and ice of the approaching winter.

When I arrived, she was tending to a fire on which she boiled water in a black earthenware pot. She was tiny, wrapped in bulky rags and sackcloth. And she was dirty, matted graying hair falling around a face that was a mass of wrinkles. She looked at me expressionlessly, as if she had been expecting my call and had no feelings about it either way.

"Madame Drouz?"

"That's right." She stopped tending the fire and stood to face me, wincing as she straightened, her hands going to support the small of her back.

"I am Magistrate Henry Aubert from Geneva. You have been named as a suspected witch. What say you to the charge?"

"I may look like a witch, sir, and I am not surprised by your visit. But I am innocent of any charges." She continued tending the fire, and I wasn't sure what to ask next. She seemed exhausted with life itself.

"May I ask, Madame, how do you live?"

She motioned to the bundles of branches piled against the one decent stone wall of her house. "I carry this firewood into the village and sell it. A few people buy. A few give me food. A few spit on me. I used to have a cow, but it died. I have my suspicions."

"What do you mean? Someone killed your cow?"

"I am not a witch myself, but there is witchcraft in these parts, make no mistake. One morning, back before the summer, I heard noises outside, and when I came out, I saw that Devil child running into the woods. Soon after, the cow started to behave like she was possessed. I couldn't milk her, couldn't control her. Then, after a few days, she just keeled over and died. I was afraid to eat her meat, but what else was I to live on?"

"The Devil child. Do you mean Clauda Rey?"

"That child should never have been born. Such deformities are curses from Hell. It was the nun, Louise, who delivered her just after she arrived in the village, ten years ago, was it? And nothing has been the same since."

"Madame Drouz, have you ever attended a Sabbath?"

"No, but I have heard what goes on. Feasting and fornication and all manner of debauchery. Do I look like someone who would be welcome there?"

I must admit, she does not.

Claudine and Clauda Rey also live apart from the rest of the village, although not as remotely as Madame Drouz. Their job, perhaps inherited from Madame Rey's deceased husband, is to operate the sluice gates of the dam channeling water towards the mill. It also appears to control the fast-flowing river so boats can more easily pass down the Rhone.

When I arrived, the mother was hard at work, preparing to wind a heavy rope intended to open the gates for a waiting fishing wherry. She called out some instructions, and I saw a small creature scamper across the top of the precarious wooden gates to the other side of the river, where it took hold of another rope. When I looked closer, I recoiled in shock, for it was not an animal but a human—albeit one that had been placed together all wrong. It was a girl on all fours, with a humped back and a matted blond head hanging at a terrible angle.

Mother and daughter strained as one to open the gates, and as the wherry glided through, the oarsman tossed the mother a coin. I wondered whether the job was a blessing or a curse; a tollgate may be lucrative, but it looked very dangerous. One false move, one slip, and the child would be swept away with the current. What mortal unease that girl provoked in me; sailors must imagine they are entering the River Styx itself when such a devilish being greets them.

Gates closed again, she half-crawled, half-galloped to her mother, who had the same face, yet her body had been placed together perfectly. Madame Claudine Rey was beautiful. She lifted the child, who I estimated to be around ten years old, as if it were nothing, and together, they formed a sort of two-headed creature. She stood in front of me with the defiance of one who had spent ten years facing down witchcraft accusations and somehow survived. She did not even give me a chance to speak.

"If you are here for my child, sir, you will not take her. She is not a witch. She has a heart of gold; you will see if you take the time."

"I am here for both of you, Madame."

At this, the woman stiffened, the child clung to her tighter, and they both looked around as if expecting soldiers to appear or to consider running. I held up my hands; I had spoken too quickly. "Just to ask you some questions, for now. You have been named as attendees at a witches' Sabbath."

"Of course, we have. But I have never been to a witches' Sabbath, sir. I am a godly woman. You can ask Pastor Bernard. He says that me and my daughter are God's children as much as anyone else, and we will have our reward in heaven."

The final named suspect, Jeanne Valleron, I left for last, no doubt putting off my encounter with a plague-spreader as long as possible. For how could she be not guilty too? There is no smoke without fire.

The woman lives on the outskirts of the *mandement*; plague-workers are supposed to isolate themselves from the rest of the community, so they live apart in little colonies. This one is particularly beautiful, the little cluster of houses well-built and well-kept, although there is no doubt it will decline with only Madame Valliez there. Only another set of plague-workers would want to colonize it after such a family.

Despite the misery and terror of their work—or, in fact, because of it—they tend to live better than the average person. The city is generous and grateful for their service; they are braver than soldiers, for who else would walk into the mouth of Hell? The answer is few. Plague-workers, *cureurs* and *cureuses* as we call them, transport and bury the bodies of the dead, then clean the empty houses. They take holy oaths to dutifully carry out their work and stay away from the rest of the community. If they die as a result of their work, their families are taken care of by the city.

To prolong outbreaks—since their livelihoods indeed depend on the plague continuing to rage or to steal from the houses of the dead. Some do it to provide for their children—a sacrifice of their life, but a risky one since many of their children die too. Others do it for reasons so murky that the idea can only have come from the Devil. Plague-spreaders annihilated my family, so it was hard to feel any sympathy for the widow, hard to feel anything but a burning desire for revenge. And if I, a godly city magistrate, feel it, how could I possibly blame anyone else for feeling the same?

Jeanne Valleron was almost skeletal, her cheekbones achingly prominent below sunken black eyes, and every time she coughed—which she did almost constantly—I thought her bones might shatter. She invited me into her home, but I declined, and we spoke outside.

"Do you live here alone?"

"Everyone else is dead."

"My family are also all dead by plague. We were victims of plague-spreaders."

We stared at each other. "And my family were victims of plague-spreading rumors. There's no such thing, you know. Of course, people make mistakes—break curfews, don't clean the houses of the dead properly—but this notion that people go around painting door handles with poison. It doesn't happen."

"Madame, there has been trial after trial, confession after confession. There are conspiracies everywhere."

"Confession." She laughed bitterly, which caused her to convulse in a coughing fit. It did not look as if she would last much longer herself, and I instinctively kept my distance.

"Madame, have you ever attended a witches' Sabbath?"

"No, but I have heard of them. And I have seen lights in the sky, the fiery tails of the witches' broomsticks. I have heard that they ride with devils."

"How do you live, Madame? How do you exist?"

"That is the question, isn't it, sir? Do I live, or do I exist? I beg. I go into the village and beg, and sometimes people throw me a few scraps—usually the pastor or Louise. But mostly, they avoid me or spit on me, and I curse them. I curse them and their families and the day they were all born—does that make me a witch? Does it?"

It rather did, in fact, according to the *Malleus*. But I was alone and not in a position to make an arrest, particularly of someone I did not want to touch. She seemed to be expecting me to arrest her, though and stood still with her hands out as if waiting for them to be tied.

"So, your family is all dead, my family is all dead, and yet here we are. What made us so special, you and I? Why did God spare us then?"

I had no answer.

I left Jeanne Valleron and headed for the river that would lead me back to Peney. On a stony beach, I untied my horse and led her to the water to drink. It was spectacularly beautiful there. We were at the foothills of the Jura, at the very edge of the canton of Geneva—the very edge of my world. Behind me, the green peaks rose into crags and cliff faces, so impossibly clear that I could trace every contour of rock, every stone and piece of rubble thrust by some giant hand, scattered onto the steep green plains. I wondered how long it would take to reach those cliffs, whether anyone had ever done it, and whether a horse could make it. I would never try, of course, because those mountains belong to Savoy—they are enemy territory.

The sun's position meant I had to squint when I turned back to the river. It was fast-flowing there; nobody would dare swim, or they would be swept towards the main Rhone, where they would be dashed against the rocks. I stood on yet another of those pebble beaches, but the other side of the river was a tangle of thick woodland, which rose dramatically to more rocky cliff faces. Though smaller, they were somehow more dramatic, more enticing, more ethereal, as the quality of light rendered them dark, blurred, and soft, like a rough painting, a sketch. I knew the city of Geneva lay beyond. A lone falcon soared overhead. It was all so beautiful that I had a desperate urge to share it with someone. I wondered how I could contrive a meeting with Louise there and decided to trace my way back to the village along the river so I could join the Nant d'Avril at some point and perhaps see her by chance.

But then I saw a church of which I had not been informed. I was struck by the need for prayer, for guidance. However, as I approached, I saw that it was one of those Catholic churches that had been abandoned rather than converted. I could see the signs of iconoclasm from far away—beheaded statues, whitewashed frescos, an overgrown churchyard path, and a tumbledown wall. It looked like a church from maybe two or three centuries ago, attractive in its way and simple enough that it could easily have been converted to the new faith. Indeed, all Genevan churches should have been converted, but with such population loss due to plague, perhaps there is no longer sufficient congregation here. The door was open, and I almost forgot to be careful with the handle.

Inside was a mess of half-finished whitewashing and rotting or absent pews. But something felt recently used. I could smell the remnants of human beings, a stale body scent perhaps, traces of animal excrement, fish...and something else... I could smell the pungent tallow of recently lit candles. I was surprised the candlesticks had not been looted with the other items. Congealed tallow dripped down their sides, and their wicks were blackened as if they had been used recently. Had a Catholic mass taken place there? Heresy of the highest order... or was I imagining it?

I sat in one of the remaining pews. There was evidence of—was it evidence? There is something going on in the village that isn't quite right, but I can't yet put my finger on it. I wondered about those women. If I hadn't mentioned the accused to each other, would they have said the same things? Did I put thoughts in their heads? Or merely tease out what was already there? Were we concocting our own narrative, and did it matter? If thoughts are sins, then surely all of us... No, this is not a fruitful avenue to explore.

It could not be denied that their stories corroborated each other. None of the women admitted to attending a Sabbath, but they all knew about the Sabbath activity with which we are all terrified and enthralled. Where could they possibly have gotten their information had they not attended the same event? All the details are in the *Malleus,* of course, but these illiterate women could not possibly have read it. Something is going on, and I am skirting around the edge of it.

The pastor's words rang in my head: You do realize that these five are all women with whom she has quarreled? There is undoubtedly the possibility that it is all rumor, gossip, and jealousy. But, as Calvin says, there is no smoke without fire. It is my sacred duty to fight the Devil, my civic duty to investigate, and my professional duty to please Calvin. This is such an opportunity. And, if women's nature is to accuse and sabotage each other, then they only have themselves to blame for the outcome. Everything that happens is God's will, and He will guide me.

I left the church and followed the stream as best I could, the horse happy to splash in the water every so often until I found a clear path onto the bank. There was rustling in the trees to one side, and I saw a squirrel dart across the path. Something crossing over my grave. And, of course, there she was. Did I know that was the path leading to her house? Perhaps I did. And what of it? I am conducting an investigation.

She turned a corner coming along the path, and almost bumped into the horse, gasping in fright as she looked up at me. "Oh, Magistrate. You startled me."

"My apologies. I did not think anyone was here."

"That is how things are in a village. There are far fewer people than in the town, but you are never alone. You will not find solitude here." She petted the horse. "Are you lost, sir? Because this is not the way back to the village..."

"I... Yes, I suppose I am lost then."

She smiled. "Come, I will show you a better way back. If you wish, that is."

"Yes, thank you." I dismounted and tried to walk beside her, as it felt like the appropriate thing to do, but, in truth, I did not know. And the path was too narrow, so she walked just in front of me. My heart was beating fast, and I was sweating, yet I somehow felt this had been the plan all along. I was being swept along like the current of the river. We walked in silence for a few minutes, and I wanted to speak, but with her walking quickly in front of me, it was even more difficult.

I opened my mouth a few times before the words came out as an awkward yell. "What are you doing out here today?"

"Fishing. At this time of year, the trout and salmon are making their way upstream to spawn in the calmer pools, so I am hoping for a good catch. I should have been here early this morning, but...I wanted to check on the prisoners."

I winced at her mention of them.

She seemed to sense my awkwardness and returned to her talk about fish. "Yes, I shall sell some to Madame Rolette at the inn, then smoke the rest for the winter. If I am lucky enough to get some roe, they make for an excellent salve for skin conditions." She went quiet again, perhaps regretting having brought up her knowledge of healing.

Meanwhile, the landscape unfurled around us in steep, rocky banks covered with clinging spiky bushes and tantalizing grassy knolls lying beyond the impenetrable vegetation. The land rolled unpredictably as we moved in and out of shimmering wooded copses, veering closer, then further from the water, following the curve of the river. Our eyes squinting then widening over and over; I felt dizzy and drunk with it all.

We emerged at an astonishing confluence of waters. Both wide and fast-flowing, one river was bright green and crystal clear, so clear I could see the details of its rocky bed, and the other was thick and gray. The waters ran alongside each other yet did not mix at all. Two rivers and two speeds—the gray rushing faster than the green, indeed at such a shocking speed that it seemed it would pull you under should you so much as dip a toe or finger in. It was one of the strangest things I had ever seen, and it was hard to believe my eyes.

"What is this place?" I asked. "It looks like there are two rivers that don't mix—how can that be? Am I mistaken in what I see?"

She laughed kindly. "Have you never seen the Junction? Despite spending your whole life in Geneva? This is the point where the rivers Rhone and Arve meet."

"Yet they do not meet."

"They do eventually, further downstream. But, here, perhaps the waters are too different. The Arve is the green water coming from the lake. The Rhone has come all the way down from the Alps. It is quite magical, isn't it?" She shrank away, face falling, for she had said a dangerous word that hung between us like a swinging ax.

"Well, we can't explain all the beautiful things on God's Earth, can we?" I said quickly and thought it a success because she relaxed and began setting up her fishing lines and net.

"I cannot believe I have not been here," I said, thinking about all the things I had missed out on, things that may have been within my grasp all along.

"It is rather inaccessible, I suppose. I first saw this place when I... well, when I made my escape, shall we say. During the exodus of the Poor Clares, you know, when I slipped away. I followed the edge of the river until I found a narrow place to cross down by Dardagny. The weather was so terrible that day; the river made waves that crashed above my head. Hard to imagine it on a day like this, of course. But it was all I could do to stay upright in the wind. At one point, I fell hard against a rock and, for a moment, feared I had broken my leg. I still have the scar today." She trailed off, rubbing her hip as if it still smarted.

"I remember that day very well."

"You do? Well, I suppose the whole city turned out to watch."

I was in the crowd that day in 1536, watching the procession of

Poor Clares as they were escorted from Geneva under armed guard. They had been counseled, persuaded, cajoled, and harassed with increasing vehemence over several years. Icon-breakers had been allowed to invade their church and cloisters; children, in particular, were encouraged, and I confess I was one of them, obtaining many books for my collection. The Sisters had been compelled to listen to Reformist preachers and explain their intransigence; husbands had been found for all of them, and two accepted to marry. The women's situation within the city walls was made untenable, and they were offered sanctuary at the vacated monastery of Annecy, a thirty-mile walk across the border.

Those pitiful eighteen sisters, some old and frail, some little more than children, were seen out of Geneva by the city's every available soldier. The streets and bridges were lined with helmets, armor, and halberds—even the cannons were manned—so determined was the city to make its point: no heretic would be tolerated in the new city of God. It had rained solidly for days before the exodus, and the bitter local wind known as La Bise had whipped up overnight, so icy gusts bit at the women as they huddled together in the streets.

They had been given shoes to aid their journey, but not knowing how to wear them, they had tied the shoes around their waists and gone barefoot, as they always had. I remember their habits whirling around them. One lost hers to the wind; she grabbed for it, but it was gone. She was left clasping at the tufts and wisps of short hair in shame as the crowd laughed and jeered. "She looks like a witch!" "She's a heretic. What's the difference?"

Why do I harden at women's shame and degradation? Perhaps because of their power. Even now, I like to think of that moment. But then I was imagining an alternative past, a daydream I knew I would enjoy returning to in the evening. I was just a face in the crowd that day, but now I wished that I had looked out for Louise, had caught her eye, and perhaps even been the only one to spy her as she slipped away to pursue her own course.

Perhaps I might have found her cowering in an alley and taken her to my house under cover of darkness, all while reassuring her that I would not betray her to the authorities. She would have lived in my house until we were of age, and then we would have married, and the authorities would have approved of my converting her. But these were pleasant fantasies I could return to later when properly alone.

I felt that I could tell her anything; I wanted to tell her everything. No, that's not quite true. I could not tell her about my private night thoughts any more than I could tell the pastor. But surely, we all have these thoughts? Surely, we all have the same heart? Even her? I wondered if she had the same imaginings. Worse, even. The *Malleus* is confirmed by so many other texts that tell us of women's lustful natures. I wonder if she has ever thought of the activities I have read about. Almost all my books are religious texts, so I'm sure she has seen them too. When I am tempted by these images, I debase myself, but if women are as insatiable as the books claim, if they truly want these things—and how could they have been invented otherwise—then she would not see it as debasing herself. If only she would make a move because I truly could not. I shook myself back into the moment and decided to try beginning one of the conversations I had constructed for us the night before.

"Do you ever feel trapped?" I asked. "You have read books about stars and the sun, you have met travelers with tales of the Orient, and you have witnessed the miracle of birth over and over. Yet, here you are, out of the cloister perhaps, but hemmed in between these mountain ranges and rushing rivers and forests. Amongst these small-minded people."

She looked amused. "You have thought about this a lot, sir?"

"No, no, I... just..." Why must I always give myself away?

"There are good and bad people everywhere," she said. "Sometimes, I wonder if our great reformers are the small-minded ones. I have learned a lot from the people here. In answer to your question: no, I have never felt trapped. Even when I was in the convent, really, it is all a matter of perspective. Did you see the beautifully painted chest in my parlor?"

"The one with the village scene and the ornate wood carvings? Yes, it was quite remarkable."

"It belonged to my father. The detail is so fine; a whole world to discover within one small picture, all surrounded by intricate carvings.

Such love and attention lavished on one small object and such pleasure to be had from it—just as much as from a cathedral or a palace. It is the same with life. Whether your canvas is large or small, there is detail and beauty, and love to be found everywhere. We only have to be open to it. Open the gates of our fortress."

"I have never thought of it like that." I had built a fortress within a fortress within a fortress—my mind within my house within my city.

"The only way in which I am trapped is in being a woman. I am afraid. I have no rights. I am in constant worry that my house will be taken from me."

"I know that fear."

"How so?"

I should not have spoken then, but I had kept it to myself for so long, and I desperately wanted her to feel sympathy for me. "After my family died, I lived alone in the family house on rue Tabazan."

"For how long? Why did you not go to the orphanage?"

"The orphanage is in the hospital, and I was mortally afraid of plague. I went to the school every day, but I told everyone a different story. Antoine Froment was my teacher, you know."

"Of course. Wasn't he everyone's teacher?"

"You say that with some bitterness?"

"Oh no, I'm sorry. It's just that his wife Marie Dentière and I are... old adversaries, let's say. She did her best to persuade me to renounce my vows."

"She tried to offer me a home. I...I...did not feel myself deserving. I blamed myself, I do blame myself for..." My voice cracked, perhaps from the late summer pollen, so I stopped. "In any case, I somehow slipped through the cracks. It wouldn't happen now, I imagine, now that Calvin has established a system of welfare."

"Now that he keeps such an intolerably close watch on everyone, you mean."

I detected criticism in her voice and said, perhaps too haughtily, "He is a great man."

She smiled in apology. "Yes. I was just teasing. And perhaps you needed someone to keep a closer watch on you. What a poor boy, living alone. And how did no one turn you out of your house?"

"There were—are, in fact—many empty houses in that area, left vacant by the departing Catholic clergy. So, it was not that unusual. In the chaos of the new administration, I managed to slip through the net."

"What a strange way to grow up. I am sorry for you. It explains why...why you are so..." She stopped herself.

I knew what she was thinking—what everyone thought: it explains why he is so aloof and quiet.

But she changed the subject slightly. "How did you live? How did you do for food?"

"My father always distrusted the banks. He kept his money stashed in a chest under the floorboards. It was a lot and in multiple currencies. Used sparingly, it lasted me until I was aged sixteen and able to use the remainder to buy an apprenticeship to a notary. My greatest fear, other than the plague, of course, was that they would change the currency or there would be inflation."

I did not tell her that I would also steal—food, clothes, books. A slight, quick boy, darting between market stalls, could take anything he wanted. Sometimes, I dared myself to be caught, perhaps even willed myself to be caught, but I never was.

"I suppose it's easier to be alone in a crowd," she said. "Alone with your thoughts, night after night, all those years. How sad...and yet there is something remarkable, romantic, about it. You are not like anybody else."

I felt hot, and it was wonderful. You are just like me, I thought. You see me, and with you, I finally see someone too.

We slowed down, and Louise led me to a flat, rocky bank where the water was deep and dark blue. "This is where I will fish, and I must get to work. If you follow the path we were just on, you will eventually reach the Peney crossroads. You know, where you must have arrived the other day, only coming from the other direction."

I was struck with a sudden desperation—I didn't want our time together to end. "Perhaps I could wait for you here. Help you carry your catch."

She looked around warily. On the other bank, far away but well within sight, two young boys were casting their own fishing lines.

Nearby, two young women were approaching with baskets of linen to wash.

"It would not do for you to be seen here, sir. As I said, one is never alone in these parts. People talk. And, when people talk, it is usually not for the good."

"I am not ashamed to be seen with you."

"But perhaps I am ashamed to be seen with you. When this is over, you will go back to the city, but this is my home. If people believe I am collaborating with a witch hunter, they will no longer trust me. And yes, perhaps they need me more than I need them, but I still have to live."

I am ashamed to be seen with you.

I have yet to end our encounters anything other than agitated.

❦ 7 ❦

TURPITUDINEM

SEPTEMBER 11, 1545

Last night, exhausted after my long ride and the day's events, I instantly fell asleep only to be disturbed by vivid dreams. I tossed and turned and fiddled with my pillow and blanket, hardly awake yet not properly asleep, my body agitated and my mind a blur. Visions came and went; Louise turning from her gardening to smile at me, saying something impossibly kind, but then turning from her patient—my victim—with anger. With disappointment that I wasn't the person she wanted me to be. Then her dark silhouette against the tree line in the forest, towering above me and flanked by squirrels. I hold the power of life and death in this village, yet she has such power over me. Then the visions turned to scenes of the prison, Darnex's screams and the snails crawling over his wounds, his wife's weeping.

I went back over all my conversations with Louise, with Bernard, and with Donzel, trying to remember every word and analyze where I might have gone wrong or right, re-imagining them as more successful conversations. The conversations mingled with the prison scenes so that I did not know what I had really done or really said at all, and nothing seemed quite real. Which was comforting, I suppose, imagining I had not really done these things, had never come to Satigny. But then, I would never have set eyes on Louise.

Downstairs, the last drinkers were being cast out into the night, and I could hear Madame Rolette bolting the doors and shutters. On my first night, there had been a gentle but insistent knocking at my door shortly before I went to sleep. I had known it to be Rolette's daughter, as she had told me she would knock, and had lain still, hardly daring to breathe, until I heard her tiptoe away. I had prayed silently to St. Anthony for his strength when he was alone in the abandoned tomb, and demons were knocking down the walls.

Since that night, Pernette had not tried to knock, although I had half-waited for it, if only to test myself. But last night, just as I thought of it, there was the knocking again. So agitated was I that, in one movement, I hurled myself from bed, opened the door, and dragged her inside, shutting it so that she almost fell against it. She had been draped in the doorway and not prepared for the violence of my movement; indeed, I had not been prepared for the violence of my movement.

But, once she had recovered from her shock, her eyes narrowed with lust, and a smile crept across her face. "Not so chaste after all then, sir?" she said as she placed a hand on my crotch.

If I am to consider even the possibility of a future wife, perhaps it would not be correct for me to be completely inexperienced in these matters. Temptation is normal, temptation is good, and even St. Augustine was fully versed in these matters—indeed one might say he over-indulged—before he became chaste. Surely, I cannot fully embrace premarital chastity if I do not know exactly what it is I am giving up.

So, I let my thoughts give way to emotions and allowed her to move closer so we were chest to chest, and I could feel her breasts pressing against me and taste her breath. Since I was a small child, I had not been so close to another person, and I wished it was not Pernette, who smelled of ale and sweat and fish. She had put rouge on her lips and white powder on her face in an attempt to look like a city lady, but the effect was comical and served to highlight the marks of childhood smallpox. The hand pressed against my crotch began to rub forcefully, the other pressed to one of my buttocks. My hands were limp and useless at my sides, and I felt I should do something, so I ripped off her bonnet. It caught awkwardly at first, but then her hair tumbled around her shoulders in beautiful fair locks that reminded me of Louise, and at that moment, the crisis came, and I shuddered.

She stepped back. "Oh, you have already..."

I decided to mask my indignity with dominance. I thought perhaps even aggression would be appropriate. "And now, what will you do?" I said, standing firm before her.

"Oh, there's more where that came from, is there?" She led me to the bed. "Lie down then."

She writhed above me... The hair... The smell... It was so present, so real, and I didn't want it, oh how I didn't want it. I tried to picture my favorite images from my books, but I desperately wanted to be alone... Who would choose the flesh of another when one's own flesh will do? I felt nothing but revulsion for myself and for her. I looked to the saints to save me from the mortification and thought of St. Thomas Aquinas, who chased a prostitute away with a flaming torch.

"Desist!" I did not mean to throw her off so forcefully, but she fell to the floor and cried out. I leaped from the bed, my breeches still undone, and took a log from the fire, brandishing it in the air.

She scrabbled to the door, picking up her discarded bonnet and stockings on the way. "This will cost you extra, Magistrate! You will pay my mother in the morning!"

Why was I unable to do what every man seems to want to do? With a woman that every man other than me seems to think is desirable? What sorcery prevented me? For a while, I tried to relieve myself, thinking of all the worst things, throwing caution to the dogs. But eventually, I gave up and curled inside my blankets, first on one side and then tossing to the other. The pillow was wet—my eyes were streaming, and I feared that maybe she had poisoned me with some foul yet scentless and colorless powder that caused them to smart. Finally, I drifted into another fitful sleep.

It was still pitch dark when I was awoken by yet more knocking, but this time, forceful banging, accompanied by a male voice shouting, "Magistrate! Magistrate! Wake up!"

I opened the door to find one of the prison guards. "Yes, what is it? What has happened?"

"It is Susanne. Susanne Darnex. She has taken ill. She has hurt herself."

I desperately didn't want to go back to that prison, and certainly not in the middle of the night, so I considered whether it could be handled without me.

Then he said, "We took the liberty of calling for Mistress Louise."

I left a suitable pause before nodding. "Go ahead. I'll dress and follow you."

In the pitch dark, it took me some time to saddle the horse, and I was not inclined to expect any help from Rolette or her daughter, who had no doubt already reported our tryst to her mother. Fortunately, there was enough moonlight to guide me, and I could see the guards' lamps in the distance as I made my way to the prison.

Another pitiful scene awaited me. I passed the prostitute's cell first, where she was cackling hysterically, and I could vaguely sense her dancing around in the dark, her ankle chain clanking. But, from the Darnex's neighboring cell came whimpering and hushed voices, and I squinted into the dim candlelight to ascertain the scene. One wall was smeared with fresh blood, and below it lay the body of Susanne Darnex.

I could see she was alive, but barely. Her forehead was a mess of exposed flesh, with blood trickling into one eye, the other slightly open. Crouching over her was Louise. On the other side of the cell, the husband sat hugging his knees and crying. There was an odd peace about the scene as if it was a painted church fresco before they were all whitewashed.

"What happened?" I asked, and everyone looked at me. I felt conspicuous, useless.

Darnex cried, "She was dashing her own head against the wall! I couldn't stop her! With these damned chains... I was begging her to stop. She has lost her mind in here!"

Louise looked up at me, and there it was again—that accusatory expression. "You have done this to her!"

At first, I thought she meant the husband. Then I realized she meant me. "What do you mean? How dare you? I wasn't even here."

She rose gently from Susanne's side and stormed towards me. "She was desperate, driven mad with it. She was trying to kill herself; can't you see?"

"But why? I told her—"

"Banishment can be a fate worse than death for some! Where would they go? How would they live?"

"I... I am sorry for them."

"I know you are. But sorry does not help. This was a woman of value, a woman needed by this community. And now she has been destroyed. A family destroyed."

This was unfortunate, and I cursed... I don't know what or who I cursed. I cursed Calvin for wrenching me out of my safe, comfortable life into this agony. I hoped it was not too late for me to salvage relations with Louise. "Will she live?"

"Yes, I think so. But she may not be the same. She is delirious at the moment. We will know more by tomorrow about which of her faculties she will regain. You may go. You are of no use here. I will stay."

I opened my mouth to object, but there was nothing to say, so I allowed her to take over. I am learning that there are times when it is best to take people at their word and times when it is best not to think too much.

8

INCURVATUS IN SE

SEPTEMBER 12, 1545

Sunday, and the atmosphere in church this morning was noticeably tenser. As people made their way up the hill in groups, the chatter was hushed and urgent. The Darnex children were there, escorted by Rolette, Pernette, and a group of regulars from the inn, who formed a sort of protective barrier around them. No doubt word had already got around about my interviews the previous day and perhaps also about their mother's injuries. God forbid people knew about my midnight tryst—surely Rolette and her daughter would not be so indiscreet.

I hung back from the crowd, planning to sidle into the church last, but when I did, almost every head turned—the room filled with whispers and mutterings that Pastor Bernard had to quell. From the front of the church, he looked at me meaningfully, although I could not tell what his meaning was. I did not feel welcome, and I may have overheard someone mutter, "How can he show his face?" But what else could I do? Attendance is compulsory. Perhaps I misheard, or they were referring to something else. In any case, there was no sign of Louise. Perhaps I should have stayed away. Do I want to be feared or liked? Can't I have both? Would I rather nobody thought about me at all, like before?

After silencing the congregation, Bernard smiled that wonderfully warm smile of his that seemed to take in and welcome every individual face in the crowd. "Next Saturday, we will celebrate the marriage of two young people of this village, Madeleine and Bastien."

With that, he instantly lifted the mood and, as if a ray of sun had shone into the church, there was a noticeable relaxing of shoulders, and the muttering turned happy, even rowdy. There was a nudging of shoulders and shy blushing glances between a boy and a girl on opposite sides of the aisle.

"Under the guidance of their parents, Madeleine and Bastien have pledged their commitment to each other. Marriage is a holy institution. Calvin tells us, 'Marriage is superior to all human contracts.' But what about desire? Is desire a sin?" He looked at the congregation expectantly but without pressure or censure. "No, of course, it isn't! All of us should be filled with desire. Desire for the Holy Spirit, desire to do good in the world. And desire within the bonds of marriage is a beautiful thing. The marital bed is a holy place."

There were giggles from the crowd. My face and ears were burning. I did not like to hear a cleric talk of such matters, to use such words. Of course, I have heard Calvin speak of them, in front of huge crowds, on numerous occasions. Not only does Calvin not shy from these very personal issues, but he has also made them central tenets of the new faith. Humans are sinful creatures, and lust is unavoidable, so it must be contained within the institution of marriage. Adultery is the "worst abomination" and is treated as such —indeed, the punishments for sexual crimes are becoming more and more severe. Trials for *paillardise*—crimes of a sexually immoral nature—have been on a steep increase ever since Calvin's return to Geneva.

Calvin is directing people's lives toward his godly society, so I can accept that he addresses it. But something made me wince internally at hearing Bernard speak of carnal matters, even as delicately as he did. Perhaps because of Bernard's naivety—Calvin, at least, was already married and had therefore experienced the pleasures of the flesh. But Bernard—in his earnestness—could only be thinking of his own future, his own desires. And if that meant Louise...

He continued. "But there are different types of desire, and some of them are sins. Who has heard of concupiscence?"

There were more titters and some groans.

"Yes, I know. I've said it before, and I'll say it again. Concupiscence is sinful lust. We always long for forbidden things and desire what is denied us. But, if we allow our baser desires to run unchecked, we will be consumed by them. Do not allow sensual folly to assume domination over your free will, your free will to transform the human bondage to sin.

"Not all are lucky enough to be married. Some have lost their spouses; some have not yet found them or never will. So how should we control our baser desires so they do not fester and rot in our souls? The answer is..."

And, as he said it, several people muttered the words along with him in unison, with a teasing faux weariness, indicating that it was one of Bernard's favorite topics.

"*Incurvatus in se.* The inward turn towards oneself. When we turn away from community, we turn away from God, as Adam and Eve did when they put their selfish desires above all else. This is what St. Augustine tells us when he talks about the difference between the City of Man and the City of God. In the City of Man, it is misdirected self-love that results in competition, wars, quarrels, and destruction. Humanity turns in on itself. But, in the City of God, we can 'dwell together in everlasting peace, in a place where self-love and self-will have no place, only a ministering love that rejoices in the common joy of all'."

He walked up and down the central aisle, looking at each member of the congregation, taking the hands of some. "The Devil is in all of our souls, and it is our godly duty to hold him back. We can all do it." He reached Claudine and Clauda Rey and smiled as he ruffled Clauda's hair, and she squirmed affectionately. "Little Clauda serves our village when she darts across the bridge and opens the sluice gates for boats to pass, boats that bring us trade. And what would you do, Clauda, if you saw the Devil sailing towards your gate, in his fiery boat, with demons manning the oars..." He laughed at himself as he tried to imagine the Devil's boat. "Would you let him through, Clauda?"

The little girl shook her head proudly, and her mother kissed her.

"That's right, Clauda," he said. "We must close the sluice gates that protect us from our darkest thoughts!"

He continued walking, reaching my place in the back pew, and I wanted and did not want him to take my hand, and he did not. "And so, I say unto you, look to your neighbor. What can you do for him? And do not look for thanks, for your thanks will come from God. Reverse the inward curve. *Incurvatus in se.*"

Incurvatus in se—there it is again. Live your life outwards. For others. I know that I live my life inwards. I have no community. My mind is my friend, my community. But, until recently, I had managed on my own, on the whole, to suppress my desires. Then this case, this *Malleus*, this village, sent them to the forefront of my mind. I feel like a loaded cannon.

9

ALTERIUS NON SIT QUI SUUS
ESSE POTEST

SEPTEMBER 13, 1545

In the morning, I approached the prison with trepidation, dreading to imagine the condition of Susanne Darnex. But she was not there; only her husband and Blaise, forlorn in their respective cells.

"Does Madame Darnex live?" I asked the guard.

"Aye, she lives. She is being nursed at home by Mademoiselle Louise and her children."

I felt immense relief, partly that I did not have to look at the injured woman, but mostly that the moment when I become responsible for a death had still not arrived. Although it looms ahead of me, a shadow on the horizon.

Darnex and Blaise were loaded onto a cart to be taken to Geneva— the man because he could not yet walk with his injured feet, the prostitute because she could not be trusted to walk obediently. I followed at a fair distance behind the horses and guards, so I could be at peace.

But Blaise, buffeted repeatedly against the back of the cart, seemed determined to engage me in conversation. "What's your pleasure, sir? You come to me in the prison in Geneva, and we can do whatever you want. I bet you ain't been with many women—I could show you a few things." She seemed only half-awake, her laughter weak and veering between coughing and tears.

Next to her, Darnex's eyes were closed, and the guards up front could not hear over the noise of the wheels and horses' hooves, so I ventured, "How can you do such things, madame? Such obscenities? Do you not fear Hell?"

She looked at me for a long time and suddenly seemed not mad, drunk, or debauched, but...what? Not intelligent, surely. Yet her eyes had become deep and lucid. "Do you think I wanted to do these things, sir? Do you think my first time with a man was at my instigation? I was nine years old and 'twas my own father who put me out to work. Did I like it?" She laughed a horrible, bitter laugh. "When you have debased yourself once when you have lost your shame, you are off on the path towards vice and corruption, and it may take time, but there's no going back. Your soul becomes remade, and your heart hardened until you don't know what is good anymore. You don't want what is good anymore. You want what is bad. Pain becomes pleasure. What makes others blush or shudder is what you want."

I desperately wanted her to stop talking and tried to slow my horse to drop back, but she only raised her voice.

"You mark my words, magistrate. Did you enjoy roasting this poor man's feet? Did you? You will! You can't unthink what I know you've thought!" She cackled and spluttered, and I kicked my heels to gallop on ahead so I would no longer have to look at her.

When we entered the city, the cart turned into the prison gates, and I continued to the stables, nodding towards the guards with my eyes off the cart in case Darnex or Blaise were looking at me. Having installed the horse in livery, I returned to my house, conducting my door-opening ritual even more carefully than usual since it had been several days, and who knows what pestilent evil had been placed there.

Having been granted indefinite leave from town hall duties for my task in Satigny, I had no cases to work on. I made a fire and sat down to read, but I could not concentrate. It was useless; nothing felt the same anymore.

I decided to go to the consistory to request an interview with Calvin. I could not proceed further with the investigation without his legal advice. A part of me wanted to be taken off the case. But another part of me could not imagine no longer being tied to Satigny. I was inextricably linked with the case. Calvin was not there, so I tried calling at his house, but he was occupied, and Idelette told me to come back at a later time.

At a loss, I wandered the streets. Although the plague still raged, I felt emboldened by my new adventure and found myself heading in the direction of the plague cemetery to pay respects to my family. The plague cemetery does not have crosses and headstones in peaceful rows, where one can wander and lay flowers and converse with the dead. It has pits and quicklime and cartloads of corpses being shoveled by decrepit gravediggers.

It was somehow comforting to see the piles of dead bodies. Perhaps that makes me seem like a monster, but there is an explanation. All those corpses, graying and mingled and forgotten, soon to fester and rot into crumbling bones. Bodies everywhere—swinging from gibbets, crowding in the market, in church, rolling together in the whorehouses and in beds behind curtains; when there are this many bodies, it diminishes the significance of everything. I have hidden amongst them, in plain sight, since I was a boy. Now, in the grand plan of things, any wrongdoing in which I am involved will not be noticed. It is the will of God, in any case. It is like Louise said when she spoke of Copernicus and his theory that we might not be the center of God's universe.

Louise thinks of heavenly bodies, I think of rotting corpses—no matter, it is the same idea. We are diminished, and everything that happens is God's will. That is no small comfort.

Calvin opened the door himself the next time and led me down the corridor to his office. "Ah, Henry. How are things progressing in Satigny? I hear you have brought in some prisoners. Very good."

"Yes. Although, I am not convinced all of them are guilty of witchcraft. There is undoubtedly something going on in that village. There are too many rumors of Sabbath activities, of…"

"And there is no smoke without fire, is there?"

"But I fear that some of it may be just that…rumor."

"And common rumor is almost infallible in matters of witchcraft! It means that it only takes one to denounce an infinite number of them! Do not trouble yourself too much, Henry. The trials will uncover the truth, and they will be conducted by our most experienced magistrates."

"Ah, I see." I felt relief but also a sudden panic.

Calvin misunderstood and thought I was disappointed not to be chosen as the prosecutor. "You must understand, Henry, that these will be very public events—that was the very purpose of you bringing the prisoners here. I have every faith in your abilities, but there are many lawmen here much more experienced than you. You will learn a lot by assisting with case preparation. You have already done excellent work. Pierre Tissot will be the prosecutor—he knows how to put on a good show."

"Oh no, of course. What I meant to say was that—I'm not sure whether the investigation is over. There may be more to uncover."

"Then you must continue, of course! We must root out every one. To use another firewood analogy, if I may—for lack of wood, the fire goes out. Book of Proverbs. Very good." He seemed to be indicating that the meeting was at an end, taking up a quill to get back to work, as I had his authorization to continue. But I lingered. "What is it? You seem troubled."

"Monsieur Calvin. What if... What if some of them are innocent?"

Calvin put the quill down, sighing, and I wondered if I could sense a slight irritation as if I had asked a very foolish question. "Do you know what a scapegoat is?"

I said nothing, but it appeared to be a rhetorical question.

"A scapegoat is an animal ritually burdened with the sins of others, then driven away. Leviticus. Agnus Dei. *Le bouc emissaire.* Azazel, pharmakos. Jesus Christ was, of course, our scapegoat. It is an ancient practice, far more ancient than even Christianity. And it is an honorable thing; indeed, there is nothing more honorable than to die a martyr for others' sins. Behold the Lamb of God who takes away the sins of the world."

"You mean that these women will be martyrs?"

"No, man." I believe he may have become impatient with me then. "There are witches everywhere—we are under sustained attack from

Satan, as you well know. But Satan is the arch deceiver, and so, if we make mistakes, it is understandable. It is all for the good. As you know, Satan often reveals himself as an angel of light."

I wasn't sure I understood but nodded anyway.

He continued with more energy—I do believe he was constructing a future sermon upon me. "It is our scriptural duty to root out this scourge of the Devil. For it says in Exodus: 'Thou shalt not suffer a witch to live.' And so, if we do not root out every one, are we not making war on God? If judges and magistrates do their duty, then they should no more tolerate witches than they would murderers. Indeed, I would be more inclined to pardon a murderer than a witch. Otherwise, it is an overthrow of God's service and a perversion of the order of Nature.

"Make no mistake, I do have some compassion for some of these unfortunate souls. In the Satigny case, perhaps they were weak in their grief. When does Satan in bodily shape meet some man and entangle him in his snares? When that man is in some grief of mind, or plagued by hatred toward his neighbor, or when a woman is contemptuous of her husband. Perhaps they are mad—but even thinking you have been to a Sabbath counts as witchcraft."

Good God, does that mean we can conduct sins within our own imagination? The things I have imagined!

Calvin led me to the door. "The people need a sacrifice—no, I'm sorry, that is an ill-chosen word. They need a scapegoat. Even if we make a mistake, it is better that a few unfortunate innocents burn than a single witch go unpunished. This is war, and in every war, soldiers have to die, do they not? Think on it."

He indicated for me to go down the corridor towards the front door, then said, "Ah, Henry."

I spun around awkwardly so that we almost bumped heads.

He coughed and stepped back, then handed me a book. "Here, I just wanted to give you a gift. A copy of my *Psychopannychia*. No doubt you have already read it, but this is the new French edition with a new introduction. Refutes the nefarious herd of Anabaptists who say that the soul dies or goes to sleep between death and the Day of Judgement. I'm rather proud since it was my first book. Only published quite recently, but I wrote it when I was twenty-five—younger than you! Off you go, Henry. And do not trouble yourself. Leave that to me."

I sloped home, hugging the book to my chest. Calvin told me not to trouble myself, but I am troubled. Scapegoat. I thought of the goat standing in Louise's front garden, passive or impassive, I don't know. The idea of those women as scapegoats should be comforting to me. Nobody loses. If these women are indeed guilty of witchcraft, then they die as they should. If they are innocent, then they die as martyrs, lambs of God, to cleanse us of our sins, and they will find their reward in Heaven. And scapegoating only works if we don't know what we are doing.

But surely, we do know what we are doing. Jesus's killers truly believed he was dangerous. But his apostles didn't, and God didn't. So, perhaps I am Calvin's apostle. This idea makes my chest swell with pride and provides no small amount of comfort.

We are watching ourselves do this from the outside. Reading the book with our thoughts in the margins. We are watching ourselves from a distance, watching ourselves being swept along on this wave of doctrine. Calvin as good as says we create these witches with our own tongues, and it doesn't matter. A woman's place is in the home, and if she is not there, she is fair game. In any case, I must obey Calvin, and both of us must obey God. As it says in the Book of Luke: "The servant knowing the will of his master, and not doing it, shall be severely punished."

10

PSYCHOPANNIA

SEPTEMBER 16, 1545

On Wednesday, a bitter wind whipped through the narrow streets and hit us full force as we left the city to journey back to Satigny—six guards and a large tipcart pulled by horses. La Bise is easier to bear when you are inside the city walls and protected from its cruelest blasts.

I followed, trying to shield myself from the wind a little. The lake was dotted with waves, their peaks invisible under a thick white blanket of cloud that became darker and grayer as the day progressed. It will be winter shortly when survival becomes prominent in everyone's minds.

I had dreaded the winters of my childhood. They were hard enough even before my parents died, with collecting enough firewood becoming the main preoccupation for all. You took your life in your hands every time you ventured outside, not only from the risk of frostbite or slipping on the ice but because you could be accosted and beaten in seconds for your furs or boots.

Older people talked of how the winters never used to be so cold or so long, that we were at the beginning of a new Ice Age, and that it was yet another punishment from God. People began to look to the snowy peak of Mont Blanc as His image.

After my parents died, there were some winters when I almost starved to death because it was too cold or I was too afraid to leave the house. The one saving grace of winter was that it did seem to kill off the plague.

The summers were easier; during the day, I could linger by the lake, watching the fishing boats come and go, and food was plentiful—if I didn't feel like spending my precious treasure, I was adept at stealing the odd apple or block of cheese from a market stall. So adept at being invisible, unnoticed. Living in the margins. Now, I am at the center of things—is this what I wanted all along? I was not living before; I was existing. And the irony is, now I am living, nothing seems real. Everything is spinning in the air as if it is a game.

The wind slowed our progress slightly, but we arrived in Peney at exactly the same time I had arrived less than two weeks before. The village was deserted, the church full. When we were outside the church door, the guards looked to me—even the chief guard—and I realized it fell to me to conduct proceedings. There was no avoiding it. I reminded myself that I was only doing what needed to be done, simply following orders from the council, from Calvin himself. It was not my choice.

Taking a deep breath, I opened the heavy church door and marched up the nave to the front.

Bernard, standing in the pulpit, stopped in the middle of his sermon. There was silence other than the clanking of the guards' halberds and boots as they formed a line at the back of the church, blocking the door.

I opened my mouth to speak, then remembered I had the sealed proclamation from the Senate in my bag and that I should adhere to the words I had practiced. I broke the seal, unraveled the scroll, and read, "In the name of the Senate of Geneva, I hereby arrest Leonarda Drouz, Claudine Rey, Clauda Rey, and Jeanne Valliez on suspicion of witchcraft. They will be taken to the prison in Geneva, where the investigation and subsequent trial will take place."

What happened next is something of a blur. There was silence, there was clamor, there was protest, there was resignation. There was the clasping of hands, the dragging of feet, the dragging of bodies, the crying of children, the cursing of women. Eyes to the floor, eyes to the ceiling, eyes wild, eyes wet, eyes blank. There was the silence of men.

I stood impassive as the four women were taken with varying degrees of protest. I fixed my eyes upon a single brick in the wall behind the altar so I did not have to focus on the little girl as she screamed for her mother.

I could sense Bernard trying to get to me; out of the corner of my eye, I saw his head bobbing, his hands waving, but he couldn't get through the tumult in the aisles and pews.

Then the women were gone, the door slammed, and I was left with eighty or so pairs of eyes on me. After a moment's hesitation, I turned on my heel, swung my cloak around myself, and followed with what I hoped was severity, authority.

Outside, the prisoners were led down the hill and loaded onto a waiting cart pulled by two horses. When I looked back, eighty or so heads were silhouetted on the hill outside the church, watching. No one had really spoken for them. They were not wanted, those women.

I mounted my horse and followed the procession toward Geneva. The sky had darkened ominously, and the black clouds rolling in the wind hung oppressively low.

As we passed the milestone at the edge of the *mandement*, I heard rapid footsteps and heavy breathing, and before I heard her calling my name, I knew it was her. I turned the horse around, and there was Louise running down the road, holding her skirts with one hand, her bonnet with the other.

When she reached me, she almost doubled over in a bid to catch her breath, but as soon as she could, she spoke, a hand over her heart.

I imagined it thudding and wanted to place a hand on it, to calm her myself.

"Magistrate. Please! Don't do this!" She composed herself, then her words flowed in a torrent of prepared and unprepared beseeching. "Please don't take them! You are sending them to their deaths!"

"On the contrary, they are going to trial."

"Come now. You know they will all die."

"Not necessarily... not if they are innocent. They have only to tell the truth."

"They will be tortured, and they will confess. Even if they have nothing to confess, they will come up with something. Wouldn't you? Have you ever been tortured? Don't you think you would say anything?"

"Yes. And that is why we must torture them at least twice."

Her voice was shrill, raised almost to a scream. "No! That is why we must not torture them at all!"

The miserable party ahead of us stopped and turned to watch as she continued.

"If you are labeled a witch, then that is what you become. You are forcing these women to judge themselves. If thoughts are sins, and you wish your bad husband dead, or you curse your cruel neighbor, then it happens, you might think yourself a witch. You are forcing these women to judge themselves, and how do you think women are ruled? Guilt. I have told you this before, Henry."

Henry! It was the first time she used my first name.

"They are judging their own perceived failures. A confession is simply a woman's own insecurity. You are sending them to their deaths, and deep down, you know it."

I was sitting with a straight back on my horse, and she seemed so far below me and so small and fragile. "Why have I never seen you in church?" I was attempting haughtiness, but I blurted it, so it came out as a non-sequitur. I wanted to stop her, to wound her, to regain the high ground in that dance of morals.

"What?" She looked confused, nonplussed, frustrated.

"I have not once seen you in church when attendance is compulsory. Why? You should count yourself lucky no one mentioned your name."

Why must I say nothing, nothing, and then suddenly say everything, say completely the wrong thing? Why must I reveal only those thoughts that I must not reveal?

"I..."

I expected fear from her at those ill-judged words of mine, but I got defiance.

She shook her head as if to shake off doubt, disbelief. She raised her voice again, but it was not shrill that time. It was strong. "Do not deflect my accusation with one of your own. I am a godly woman. You know very well the reasons I have not been in church—I have been taking care of your prisoners."

My only option was to be affronted, so I tapped the reins and stirrups, and the horse moved abruptly, almost knocking her over, so she had to leap out of the way.

"Wait, please! Please, my apologies! Just...please stop and hear me for a moment."

I stopped but continued looking straight ahead—to where the guards had begun to mobilize the cart and horses again. The heavens were about to open, and they were anxious to get to the city.

But Louise had the opposite in mind. "Please, come down from your horse for a moment. Do me this honor."

I dismounted and stood facing her.

She moved towards me so that we were closer than we had ever been, and I looked at the guards in embarrassment. It was beyond inappropriate. Then she touched my wrist—just briefly—but unmistakably as she looked up into my eyes. "I know you are trying to create Calvin's godly society. I know you believe that. But this is not the way. The Devil is here, yes. But not in these women. The Devil is in all of our souls." She sighed, wrung her hands, and looked around as if for inspiration. "What would you do, sir, if you were tortured? If you were on the rack, with nothing left to lose—would you reveal your true feelings?"

The rain had begun to fall in fat, individual drops, and I was vaguely aware of grumblings from the guards and wails from the prisoners. But I could only stand and look at Louise, blinking back the rain. Perhaps that was the moment I could have...should have...but I had no answer, and she grew agitated again, her face darkening.

"Your worshiped Calvin. Has he ever been tortured? Has he ever faced an impossible choice between Heaven and Hell?"

"That is precisely what he faces!"

"Come, sir. He is on a pedestal, divorced from the realities of hardship."

"It is not only poor people who know suffering."

At that, she dropped some of the anger from her tone. "You are right. I'm sorry. I...I don't want it to be you. I don't want it to be you who does this. I want it to be someone else. So that I can still feel that..."

Still feel what? I waited breathlessly as she clutched at and kneaded her cloak in agitation, looking around her as if trying to find the right words.

"Come on, magistrate!" yelled one of the guards. "It will be dark soon!"

The moment was lost, and her urgency on behalf of the prisoners returned. "Your Calvin is a coward! He would never martyr himself. Did he stay in France to face his detractors? No, he ran to Geneva, to reinvent himself as a hero. You see how he abandoned his friend Froment? People become nothing to him. You should not trust him the way you do."

"I shall forgive and pretend I never heard that."

"I do not take it back."

I swung myself onto the horse and looked back at her.

"I do not take it back! I do not take it back!" Sobbing, she fell to her knees, skirts falling around her in the mud, the rain driving by then, plastering strands of hair to her face.

I turned around on the horse a few times, indecisive, then set off after the prisoners. There was nothing else to be done. It couldn't be helped.

❧ II ❧

ODI ET AMO

OCTOBER 3, 1545

In the days since the arrest, I have been back at home in the rue Tabazan, and everything looks the same, but everything feels different. My head is filled with new thoughts, new imaginings, far closer to reality than anything that came before. I cannot decide if my heart is full or if I am even more desolate than before; all I know is that I struggle to keep Louise out of my mind. Or perhaps I do not really struggle. She is the first thing I think of when I wake, the last thing before I sleep, and there are simply not enough hours in the day to satisfy my imaginings. If I think of someone constantly, does it then mean I am in love? Or does it mean I have been possessed, bewitched? Perhaps it is the same thing. I wonder how one knows when they are in love.

In truth, I have had time on my hands these past few days since the state has taken over the reins of the investigation. I presented my evidence to Tissot and expected him to ask for my assistance, but he did not. I should have been relieved to let others take over the moral responsibility for it, but I was somehow bereft. I have been wandering the city with my thoughts, replaying in detail my conversations with Louise, agonizing over every word said and gesture made to ensure I had them exactly as they were. I analyzed each word and gesture to consider what they meant. Then I replayed the encounters as I wished they had been—if I would have said things differently, if she would have responded differently, if the conversation would have gone in other directions. I could have told her all the things I wanted her to know about me. I re-imagined them so many times that, eventually, I forgot what really happened, the awkward parts were erased, and history was rewritten the way I wanted.

After exhausting that activity, I invented new encounters. Other ways our paths might have crossed, what we might have said to each other, and how I could have made her feel about me with my words and actions. These imaginings are so pleasurable that I can't remember what I used to do with my time before Louise. And so vivid I can hardly remember what really happened and what was just fantasy. I visited the plague cemetery again, imagining a delightful scene where Louise and I would go there together. She would comfort me for my childhood losses, and we would talk at length, and I would say all the things I have never said all these years.

Surely there is nothing wrong with that? And, if there is nothing wrong with that, then perhaps my other imaginings are also harmless. Because I still need those, of course. I have more recourse to them than ever before. When I am done with my thoughts of Louise, I turn to my collection of sacred books, to the margins in particular. It is very odd that the moment I try to blend the two, my member fails me. I cannot picture Louise in my usual fantasies—she is far above that. She has truly bewitched me in the most glorious way! I feel as St. Augustine must have felt upon his conversion; unruly passion transformed into holy passion, a stallion galloping away from the fires of lust towards the heavens, for which I now thirst instead.

When St. Augustine was battling temptation, he kept his soul aloft by recognizing that "laziness is the Devil's workshop" and keeping himself busy. He preached, taught, and wrote a mass of books, homilies, and letters. St. Jerome did the same, learning Hebrew precisely because his "mind was burning with desire and the fires of lust." At this point, I could have taken on other civil cases, but I was loath to do it, my mind too occupied.

But I still took St. Augustine's advice by writing in this diary—thank God for the comfort of this diary, where my words flow so much easier than my speech. I read the *Malleus* again, from cover to cover, and I also read what other tracts on witchcraft I could obtain from the bookstall in place Molard. I purchased Johannes Nider's *Formicarius*, *A Scourge for Heretical Witches* by Nicholas Jacquier, *The Defender of Ladies*, and the *Tractatus contra daemonum invocatores*. All those books and more are written by learned scholars, prudent men, and men of God, and they corroborate each other, not to mention the *Malleus*, in the details of how witches operate. Despite the terrors documented in those books, I feel vindicated in the work I have done. I imagined visiting this bookstall with Louise, smiling and chatting together as we perused the options. She would choose a songbook by Claude Sermisy and a volume by Paracelsus, and I would allow it.

I also read the copy of *Psychopannychia* Calvin had gifted to me. It was intended as a refutation of the Anabaptist belief that the soul, separated from the body, remains dormant from death until the Resurrection. The Christian life is a pilgrimage through the world toward eternity, with death as a joyful release. There are two types of death—the separation of body and soul, which is the fate of all humans, and alienation from God, wherein the person swells in an abyss of confusion. This is the death of the soul.

Two types of death—where else had I heard about the death of the soul? In the *Malleus*, of course.

Calvin says the soul proceeds to immediate judgment—the Elect entering into bliss. Purgatory is, of course, rejected. But, if souls pass immediately into judgment, what of the Last Judgment when Christ will return to establish the New Jerusalem? Have not the souls already been judged? Several of our new church fathers have tried to find an answer to this conundrum. Luther spoke of souls falling asleep until the Last Judgment. But Calvin believes there are two judgments—the first at the end of life, the second at the Last Judgment. The souls of the faithful enter into bliss, but not fully. They remain in a state of expectation until the Final Judgment when all is revealed. Thus, for Calvin, the expectations that mark the life of a Christian continue in death.

It is a coincidence that Calvin gave me that book because I have been considering the soul a lot in recent weeks. Perhaps ever since I read that sentence in the *Malleus Maleficarum*, the one about the "death of the soul": "For the penalty of death is not inflicted except for some grave and notorious crime, but it is otherwise with the death of the soul, which can be brought about by the power of a fantastical illusion or even by the stress of temptation."

Can the soul die while we are still alive? If that can be caused by the stress of temptation, then I am sorely in danger. But I must not trouble myself too much. Humankind has been considering the soul since ancient times. I have the complete works of Plato, who tells us that the soul is tripartite, made up of Reason, Spirit, and Appetite. Reason rules, but the Spirit leads us toward good, while the Appetite leads us toward bad. If Appetite defeats Spirit, the soul will be unjust. I believe my Reason and Spirit are dominant. Indeed, I have never indulged my appetites, not with a single other human.

Walking around the city, there are constant reminders of the upcoming trials; town criers, public notices nailed to posts, and gossip on seemingly every corner. I hear the words 'Satigny', and 'witches', everywhere, and I feel gloriously connected to it all. So connected that I wished I could join in those conversations too, add some details to the gossip, even tell them I was the one, I was the one.

I write this by candlelight in the silence of the night curfew, and although it is long past midnight and sleep is still far away, I feel some relief at having finally decided what to do next. After these days and weeks of limbo, persecuting myself with questions, I realized today what was hindering me: I need to return to Satigny, because things are not finished there. I have not fully understood the place, nor completed my investigation, nor proved my worth to Calvin.

It was a particular conversation I overheard today that gave me the reason I needed to go back. Two women were chatting at a vegetable stall in the marketplace. "...and I heard that the Sabbath in Satigny is the worst of them all... such things that go on... the Devil himself has been in attendance..." The Sabbath! I realized it was the Sabbath in particular that had been bothering me; it was too much of a coincidence that all those women had mentioned strange and sinister goings-on there. And tomorrow is Saturday! Now I have formulated a plan to return to Satigny, sleep may finally come. All our best and worst plans are made in the middle of the night.

12

SPECULUM STULTORUM

OCTOBER 4, 1545

Late on Saturday afternoon, under a darkening sky, I collected my horse and left the city gates for Satigny.

"State your business," demanded the guards.

"I am a magistrate on senate business, conducting an investigation in Satigny."

"You're traveling to Satigny at this time on a Saturday? Can't it wait? There are bandits about—we arrested three yesterday. Italians, they were."

"No, it can't wait. But I know my way very well. And look, there is a full moon tonight. Thank you for your concern."

"Mind out then. Rather you than me."

When I arrived in the village, I scanned the houses for lights and signs of activity. I rode past the inn; it was busy, of course, but other than Rolette's piercing laughter, the voices were deep and male. No, any Sabbath activity would be in a secret location. And hadn't the women talked about a place hidden by trees? I headed to the hamlet of Peissy, a cluster of houses bordering the forest.

Sure enough, as I approached, I heard female voices laughing and singing, rising and falling, and saw lights dancing behind a curtained window. I was surprised because, for some reason, I had expected the witches' Sabbath to take place outdoors—but I must make no assumptions. The house was larger than the rest, with a double front, a huge barn attached, and a water wheel on the stream—the miller's house.

I tied my horse next to the fountain and crept closer. I wondered whether I should simply knock on the door, but what if it was dangerous? If there was devilish activity occurring inside, a man of God such as myself would not have been welcome—my life and soul at risk. So, I crept to the front door. Left ever-so-slightly ajar, there was just enough of a gap for me to peek inside and get a good view of what was happening. It was so dark outside I felt confident that, as long as I remained still and quiet, I would be safe. And if any women—or creatures—approached the door, I would have time to dart back against the wall.

A roaring fire in the hearth lit the large room, with thick tallow candles set on iron stands in each corner. The furniture was dominated by a large table pushed slightly back from the center of the room, which was laden with jugs of ale and plates piled with grapes, cheese, and bread.

I counted eight women and recognized some of them. Four older women were sitting on chairs, amongst them Donzel's wife and the mother of the soon-to-be-married Madeleine. She was chatting animatedly with three other girls. From their gestures, it looked as if they were discussing her wedding dress.

Each of the older women held a long stick that looked like an upended broom with thick, white wool at the top. It reminded me of the "white stick, black stick" that Blaise had chanted. They held them in one hand and, with the other, held another, smaller wooden object, which they spun rapidly. Indeed, their hands were moving so fast that they mingled with the firelight and candle flames, and the motion made me dizzy.

Madeleine put her equipment down for a moment to take a slug of wine, but she missed the edge of the table, and the stick fell to the floor with a clatter.

"Have a care, Madeleine! If you handle your husband like that on your wedding night, there won't be any little Bastiens running around!"

The older women chuckled to each other.

"Oh, but this is her little Bastien," said one of the girls, "and she will take such good care of him." She retrieved Madeleine's spindle, which was indeed bulbous with yarn and shaped like a male member. She then stroked it and caressed her face with it before sticking her tongue out to touch the tip, which caused such an explosion of cackling that I almost fell against the door and gave myself away.

"But it won't really be that big?"

"If you are lucky, it will be!"

She looked to her mother. "But won't it hurt?"

"Aye, that it will at first, my dear. But, if you have a good husband, and I believe that you will, it is something to be enjoyed eventually. And if you have a bad husband, something to be endured."

"And if you have no husband, you can use your spindle!" One of the women sat back on a rocking chair, legs splayed, skirts up, and made a gesture so obscene, I do not wish to write it down.

"I'd wager that Magistrate has a fine spindle. Such a tall and handsome man. If he wasn't such a sinister witch hunter, I should like to work his spindle."

"Yes indeed, because I'll wager he doesn't know what to do with it himself."

"I'll teach him."

"I'd put this spindle right up his arse."

"He can put his spindle up my arse. I don't mind."

So, it is true, I thought to myself, what the Bishop of Worms says. Women are insatiable, and they crave the obscenest pleasures imaginable. People really do such things.

"A city man like him? A godly magistrate with such a fine figure and face? Surely, he'd never do something so lewd."

There was raucous laughter. "She hasn't heard what happened with Pernette."

Through tears of laughter, the women recounted my exploits with Pernette in mortifying detail.

My eyes were smarting too. Perhaps it was the firewood.

"Will any of the village boys come tonight, Mother?"

Men come to such gatherings too? I looked around, fearing someone would come up behind me and I would be found out.

Too late, I realized one of the women was coming to the door. "I'll just visit your privy if I may—" The door swung open, and she almost collided with me. "Oh! It's the Magistrate!"

Our faces and chests were almost touching. She was pretty, exhilarated from her laughter, and smelled of warm bread. It was almost a pleasant moment, but two of the older women had gotten up and thrown down their sticks and spindles, and they all advanced toward me menacingly. Witches indeed!

"What does he think he's doing here?"

"He was listening at the door. And looking in, no doubt."

"Spying on us? Eavesdropping? What did you think you'd find?" Madeleine's mother waved her stick at me. "Broomsticks?"

"The shame of it. This is women's work; this is a woman's place. Go to the inn, and there you'll find some Sabbath night company."

There was nothing to say—unless I apologized, and I was determined not to do that. After all, I had every right to investigate rumors of Sabbath night goings-on. I bowed slightly and said, "I bid you good-night, ladies."

As I stepped back, I tripped over a stone and stumbled; fortunately, I managed to stay on my feet, but it was ungraceful, nonetheless. Exactly as I had done that day on Louise's garden path. And, although I did not look, I could hear snickering. I staggered back to my horse, my head spinning in confusion and shame. I had been hounded from there. What did it mean? Shouldn't they have been afraid?

I stood next to the fountain, stroking the horse's mane, turning about, not knowing what to do. It was late at night, and the weather had turned for autumn, far colder than when I had been there the previous week. It was pitch dark, and I had nowhere to go. Believing I was alone, I stamped my feet, put my head in my hands, and cursed myself, cursed the village of Satigny and all its inhabitants. The events of the past couple of weeks had been all too much. Then I realized I was being watched. Perhaps by the only person I could have tolerated seeing me in such a condition.

"Having a bad night, magistrate?"

It was Bernard, standing calmly at the edge of the square, hands behind his back. His tone was mocking but gently so and kind.

"Yes, I suppose you could say that." It was beyond mortification, so I allowed myself to embrace the vulnerability of him having discovered me, and it was a relief.

"Back in Satigny so soon? What news do you bring?"

"None, er, none. I am here on official business. I am investigating claims about Sabbath goings-on. Several of the accused women spoke of it. It can't be ignored."

Although it was dark, I could see his eyes shining with that gentle mocking.

"Have you never heard of a spinning bee?"

"A spinning bee? No, I have not."

"It is a perfectly innocent way for women to congregate. Not only that but we would not be clothed for winter without it."

"But their talk. They were... It was so unseemly."

"Be kind to them. They work hard. Why should they not enjoy their work too? While their husbands drink themselves stupid with Madame Rolette, these women are clothing the village for the winter and making their livings. Spinning is a godly activity; you know that. It denotes female virtue. Remember Proverbs: 'Who can find a virtuous woman? For her price is far above rubies...she seeks wool, and flax, and works willingly with her hands... She perceives that her merchandise is good; her candle goes not out by night, she lays her hands to the spindle, and her hands hold the distaff.'"

"But I heard them talk of young men visiting."

"Sometimes, yes. It is a suitable time for young men and women to meet under the watchful eyes of their mothers, aunts, and grandmothers." He sighed. "Magistrate. We have much to learn from Calvin about how we can contribute to the City of God. But our ways are not so bad."

I was not satisfied, still smarting from my insult. "They offended me greatly. They used me for sport."

"Well. You have not exactly endeared yourself to many people here. I think that would be a reasonable statement, would it not?"

"But they should be afraid of me. I do not understand. Why are they not afraid of me?"

Bernard became serious now. "They are afraid, believe me, they are.

So, they are fighting with everything they have. They have to stick together. Because who will fight for them when they are forced to turn on each other? Look." He looked around surreptitiously, automatically, for there was no one and nothing in the blackness around us. "The truth is there are Sabbath goings-on in this area. But it is not at Madame Perrin's spinning bee. Would you like me to show you? You will have to keep out of sight and promise not to be too scandalized."

I felt a surge of excitement. Was it what I had been searching for all along? Was the clergyman involved as well? Or, at the very least, involved in the cover-up? I may have suspected him of apostasy, of clinging to some of the vestiges of his former Catholic faith, of being too lenient with his parishioners, but I had certainly never suspected him of anything approaching diabolical activity. I tried to conceal my excitement as I said, "Very well. If there is something I should know, then you must show me."

"Come. It is a short walk from here. In an ideal world, we would have torches, but the only way I can access a flame around here is to go back to Madame Perrin's house and beg, and I don't suggest that course of action, do you?"

"But is it safe?"

"Oh yes, perfectly safe."

Why was he laughing? I still felt I was being mocked, but I did not know why. Was this the danger I had been seeking all along? I must confess I was nervous. "Should we bring provisions?"

"It is not far. There will be provisions there, although I don't imagine you will want to partake."

I couldn't read his expression—*why can we never tell what others are thinking?* —but my mind was filled with imaginings, horrible and thrilling. We left the village proper, and my heart raced as our route took us toward Louise's house. But, to my disappointment, we turned down a path in another direction, veering towards a thick forest. When it became impenetrable for the horse, I tied her to a branch.

"Mind yourself here," said Bernard, bending branches and twigs so they did not snap into my face.

It was not a pathway as such, but a way had been semi-cleared, as if people had been there before us. I soon heard noises and discerned lights. There was music—the beat of a tabor, more than one, the strumming of lyres, and a pipe melody floating above. There was singing, laughter, and twinkling lights that danced. There was the scent of delicious roasting meat, and I heard the crackle of flames, then Bernard muttering to himself, "They should not be lighting fires out here... Well, I suppose it has rained so much that the damp will protect the surroundings."

"Who is 'they'? Where have you brought me?" I was standing behind him and perhaps using him as a sort of shield.

Bernard turned, and there were those shining eyes again. "Go ahead, take a look," he said, motioning for me to pass him. "A few more yards, and you'll be at the edge of the clearing—stop there before they see you." I hesitated, but he said, "Don't be afraid. You can trust me. And I trust you."

He moved aside, and I crept slowly to the edge of the tree line. The forest thinned into a large clearing, in the middle of which burned a large fire. Around it, people were dancing wildly, flinging their arms and legs. Natural rock formations made a table and a circle of seating around which others were eating and drinking.

Another smaller fire had a spit with the remnants of a boar and its piglets, most of which had already been consumed. In corners, against trees, behind rocks, I saw snatches of white flesh; a dress pulled up here, bare buttocks thrusting there, limbs and hair and glistening skin.

"What does this remind you of?"

I jumped with fright as Bernard had moved silently behind me and spoken in my ear.

He placed his hands on my shoulders, which was comforting. "Those villagers wearing beast masks, are they not the dancing imps? And the couples enjoying each other, the copulating demons? Those roasting piglets, do they not look a little like human babies? And there —a boy riding on a cow? I have heard that witches sometimes ride on animals, too, as well as riding on broomsticks. Like the witches you just saw at the spinning bee." Even though he was whispering urgently, I could tell he was somehow amused, yet I did not know why because surely it was scandalous. "If you were to stay until the early hours, you may be unfortunate enough to see old farmer Humbert enjoying his prize sow a little too much. I believe bestiality is an essential part of the Sabbath, too, is it not?”

"What is going on here? What is the celebration?”

"This is the Sabbath, magistrate. When those who have nothing can pretend they have plenty. It is a tradition that existed long before Christianity decreed it would be on this particular day.”

"But this is debauchery...”

"There is a fine line between merriment and debauchery, a fine line between pleasure and obscenity, and I do not believe either of these lines has been crossed tonight. There is no law, religious or civil, against drinking for pleasure. And those people copulating over there —they are a married couple.”

"But it is in public!”

"Not if you don't look. Look instead at these other people's faces, Magistrate. Look at their joy, their release.”

"But how can you say no lines have been crossed? Look at what they are doing! Does this happen every week?”

"Goodness me, no. But this is a precarious time of year in the countryside, Aubert. It is harvest time, and the summer has been kind, but I'm sure you have noticed the rains recently. During this precarious time, before the crops are in for the winter and the animals are down from the mountains, there is a lot of fear and uncertainty. Livelihoods are at stake; lives are at stake. It is no coincidence that these witch-craft accusations are coming now.”

"Wait...is that Donzel?”

A fat man wearing only an unbuttoned white shirt was holding court in the corner of the clearing, sitting on a high rock with legs splayed as he instructed some woman to pour ale into his mouth while others giggled and danced.

"Yes, I believe it is. The Devil on his throne, you might say. And, unfortunately, there are plenty of women in this village who have been compelled to make the osculum infame with him. I believe the Devil requires converts to kiss him on his...excuse me...on his anus, correct me if I am wrong. As a sign of their devotion. Donzel lets people off their taxes for the same price.”

"But it is unthinkable that he should be here! The village *châtelain!*”

"I can't say that I condone his cavorting or his corruption. Indeed, I strongly condemn it. He is a terrible *châtelain,* and perhaps I hope you report him. Perhaps that is why I brought you here. But it is a great leveler, the Sabbath, don't you think? And rural ways are different from those of the city of Geneva."

"But you are a part of the city of Geneva too." My expression remained incredulous, so he led me away consolingly. I could hardly tear my eyes away and secretly wanted to stay and watch, although I could not admit that to Bernard. I wanted so very much to see the osculum infame—could it really be done? So much material there, so much for me to think about when I was alone.

"Perhaps I should not have shown you. But I wanted you to know the worst that happens here. These are good people. But they have been through a lot—war, plague... There is only so much hardship people can take if they do not have some sort of release, some form of merriment. It is too much austerity that causes transgression." He continued as we made our way gingerly back through the forest, beseeching now as he feared he had not only not convinced me but made things worse. "Now that faith is reformed, the new expectations for laypeople are high. There is a heavy toll on the spirit. This new moral policing. We must allow people some leeway. They used to have Confession to unburden themselves, but now they must unburden themselves in other ways. The spiritual rigors of predestination are great. It is hard for people to comprehend Calvin's teachings about the Elect and the Reprobate, the doctrine of Total Depravity. The notion that nothing they do can have any effect on God's will. That they have no control."

"It is not a doctrine. It is the true faith."

"Yes, I'm sorry. But it must be taught as a doctrine before it becomes a part of people's lives. It will take time, Magistrate. We must have compassion. We cannot all be scholars to debate the finer points of double predestination as if we were trained orators in the consistory."

"Yes, but you know as well as I do that Calvin does not want us to give up Confession completely. We must now be our own confessors."

"It is hard to confess to yourself. To admit who you truly are.

Confession was designed to enforce religious morality, and now there is a vacuum. People can justify themselves; they can get away with it spiritually. They can be dishonest with themselves. And so, we must be honest with ourselves. We must aid people's consciences. They need steering. Because the care of their soul is too much responsibility for them to bear."

Too much responsibility for them to bear. How that phrase resonates in my bones. I am wading through the mud, sinking deeper and deeper and looking for branches to grasp. And what else did he say? It is hard to admit who you truly are? Good God, help me!

By then, we had reached the edge of the village square, where I had tethered the horse. We stopped and faced each other awkwardly, neither sure how to interpret our experience of the last hour.

"You are staying at the inn, I presume?"

"No. In fact, I came here directly from Geneva this evening on a whim, I have to admit. I have nowhere to stay. I don't imagine they would be very glad to see me at the inn, so I shall ride back to Geneva tonight."

"You can't possibly do that. For every reason—it is freezing, there is no moon, there are bandits about—I forbid it."

"Everyone is forbidding me from doing things."

"Well, that makes a change from you doing the forbidding. Come, you will stay with me. It is modest but comfortable."

A few minutes later, I was installed in the tiny parlor of the vicarage at the bottom of Peney Hill, warming myself next to the fireplace. Bernard brought us two mugs of ale, and we sat silently for a few moments. Then we heard laughing voices from outside, and I drew back the curtain to see a group of young people stumbling their way home, no doubt returning from the Sabbath. Two of them held candles that danced in the darkness in time with their bodies. Bernard smiled, and I found myself smiling, too, before I darkened the mood again.

"The city is moving to ban dancing completely," I said. "A law has been drafted. I drafted it myself, in fact."

His smile faded. "And then something will be lost."

I looked at him in surprise. A member of the clergy advocating for dancing? According to Calvin, dancing is a sexual activity that has no place in a godly society. What was he doing at all, showing me all that?

Reading my mind, Bernard said, "Pleasure is not a sin. There is a difference between fun and dissolute behavior. You must allow these people to teeter on the edge sometimes. You will find that they often make the right choices. They are exploring frontiers. If you stay away from the edge, how will you ever know what lies below? You cannot have Heaven without Hell. And so, in my view, the existence of obscenity makes apparent what is correct behavior. What is offensive is also revelatory. Even the fact that we find it offensive. This is the way we can 'civilize the body,' as Calvin puts it."

That was a comfort, I suppose. I ventured, "In your sermons...you don't shy away from these subjects. You don't avoid discussing..." I didn't know how to say the words, but he helped me.

"I don't avoid discussing the pleasures of the flesh, you mean."

I shifted, uncomfortable.

He laughed kindly. "Neither do our great reformers! Martin Luther studied the Scripture, studied families and human nature, and concluded that humans are bodily creatures with physical needs, driven to provide for these needs by desire. 'As Christ befriended, healed, fed, and washed the bodies of those he met, so too the Christian is called to human relationships with others. And that includes the bodily service of the neighbor. And that includes a wife. Procreation.'"

"So, Luther himself rejected sexual abstinence as a human virtue?"

"Yes, of course! Luther is married. Calvin is married. Fromen and Dentière are married, Farel, Viret, all. Some of the Poor Clares took husbands. I have come to believe that celibacy is not a natural state. If we suppress our natural desires, they fester and turn rotten. Just as if we do not confess our sins—to ourselves, I mean—" He quickly clarified. "—they also fester inside us and gnaw away at our souls. So, I myself would like to experience the pleasures of the flesh. It is God's will, after all." He looked at me nervously. "You must have, sir? I imagine it must be a marvelous thing."

I felt myself reddening. I was shocked by his candor and wished we were not talking about such things. I was damned if I was going to tell him the truth: that I had not so much as held a woman's hand until that infernal innkeeper's daughter defiled me. And then until Louise touched my wrist. That I preferred to take my pleasure alone. I made some sort of noncommittal shrug, on which I had no intention of elaborating. When I could avoid his eyes no longer, I looked at him, and he was staring intently.

"She will be next, you know."

We had both been thinking about Louise. Of course, we had. And I loathed him and loathed myself. I tried to look confused as if I didn't know who he was referring to.

He leaned forward, voice hardening with urgency. "If you care for her, and I can see that you do, you will do something to stop this."

How did he see through me? If he saw that, what else did he see?

"Good God, man, you can be difficult to talk to. I am trying to help you. We could be friends, you know. I don't have any friends here, in my position."

Still, I did not speak. I was considering the notion of friendship. I had not before. Again, I was struck by the possibility that things could have been different. Despite my years of imaginings—indeed, I have created every possible scenario in my mind—it is a somehow terrifying notion to consider the choices one might have had.

Bernard sighed and patted the chair arms with his hands. "It is very late. If you ever want to unburden yourself..."

"Confession?"

He flung his head back in irritation. "No, man, of course not. How many times do I have to tell you I am Reformed. I simply mean I am here to listen."

We went to our respective chambers, and I knew that he would go to sleep thinking of Louise, and I'm sure he knew I would do the same. It is hard to admit who you truly are. Perhaps that should be a comfort. We are all the same. In the morning, I was awake at first light and returned to Geneva without saying goodbye.

13

CAPUT GALEATUM

OCTOBER 6, 1545

The city felt different in the morning as I emerged from my doorway and underwent the usual doorknob ritual to the chimes of La Clémence. Our cathedral bell has these words inscribed at its base: "I praise the true God, I summon the people, I assemble the clergy, I weep for the dead, I chase the plague away, I embellish feast days. My voice is the terror of all devils."

And, that day, I hoped that devils would be afraid and that justice would be done in the hall of Mairie. There was a marked excitement in the air as I tried to weave my way toward the entrance's stone steps. Nothing you could put your finger on but a communal sense that something was about to happen. I could hear snatches of gossip:

"Apparently, the whole village is riddled with witches... I heard the Devil himself was at their Sabbath... There'll be more arrests, mark my words... All women, of course... Makes me shudder to think of those heretics brought inside the city walls..."

Sure enough, as I approached the hall, I saw a large crowd assembled, all hoping to catch a glimpse of Leonarda Drouz when she was dragged from the prison to the courtroom. Many also hoped to get a place in the public gallery to watch the proceedings, but most would be disappointed and have to wait for the *cryer* to emerge with his periodic reports.

As a magistrate, my seat was guaranteed, of course, but I had to push through the rabble to reach the entrance. I pressed my pomander against my face and tried to snake my body so it touched others as little as possible. I longed for the open space of Satigny, where I could avoid those festering bodies, and the thought of Satigny, and Louise, made me smile a little.

It was to be a public spectacle as much as a criminal trial, and the gallery was full. There was an almost carnivalesque atmosphere to proceedings, which both sickened and thrilled me. Such a fine line between the two.

The process would be that as for any criminal trial. The panel of four syndics, the leading councilmen who would decide the accused's fate, sat behind a wooden table on a raised platform at the front, with a dais for the lieutenant, who would be instructed to carry out the eventual sentence, and a wooden dock for the prisoner. All 25 members of the Small Council were also in attendance in the front rows, including myself, of course. The public galleries were packed, and the echo of excited voices chattering was almost deafening.

I looked around for Calvin, but he was conspicuous in his absence. He attends the meetings of the Consistory and Company of Pastors and, as such, knows the lives of Geneva's citizens in intimate detail, but he has no formal role in city government. He skirts around the edges of it, like me, and look what power he has.

There was a hush as the heavy wooden doors opened, and Leonarda Drouz was brought into the room backward, flanked by two guards holding her arms as she shuffled on her heels. It is customary for a suspected witch to be brought into the courtroom backward, in accordance with recommendations in the Malleus and many other learned texts, in case she should want to place a curse upon the judicial officials.

The court was opened by the Leader of the Small Council, Michel Varro, in the new customary manner. He hit the ceremonial gavel and stood to speak. "In the beginning, I pray to the Lord, Father and Author of this republic, that as He loved us, delivering us from the darkness, tyranny, troubles, and corruption so dangerous in which we are today, that it pleases Him to protect, guard, and maintain against all the enterprises of the Devil, tyrants, conspirators, the wicked and the envious. And, since we depend on Him in everything, may He also be our help and refuge. And that, by His Holy Spirit in governing the magistrates and officers of this, His republic, in such a way that really all the service, having Him always before the eyes, loving the good and punishing the bad, and acting each in His Place and all together as true servants and sent from His Majesty. Hear our prayers, Lord. By Your great kindness and mercy, we are filled with Your infallible promises. Amen."

Such comfort and beauty in these words. Such comfort to have church and state combined to bring God's justice. Everything that happened there today was not only under the eye of God but willed by Him. And not by us.

Then the trial began. The questioning of Leonarda Drouz took place in public as a morality play. And prosecuting magistrate Pierre Tissot was a fine actor in that morality play—it was his stage, and he was ready to perform. He looked almost jubilant as he rearranged his notes and cleared his throat.

I fear I will never be able to do what he does. Even if I could build the case, write the words as well as he, I could never perform them. When I can barely hold a conversation without swallowing my words, I managed to make that speech in Peney church when I arrested the women, but it gave me nightmares before and after, and the thought of it still makes my skin crawl.

There would be no defending lawyer since it was only necessary to provide a defense if the accused requested one, and how would those simple peasant women know to ask? Even if they did request a representative, no lawyer in his right mind would risk being the representative of a witch and, therefore, damned as a heretic himself.

Tissot began with a neutral—almost conciliatory—tone, asking Leonarda basic questions that I would also have done as well as he. Her name, her place of birth, her family, her means since the death of her husband... Several times, he had to ask her to speak up and wasted no opportunity to play to the crowd. "Raise your voice, if you will,

Madame Drouz! You may well commune with the Devil by means of thought alone, but we are mere mortals and, as such, have a mortal requirement to hear your voice!"

He then moved on to the accusations made by Blaise against Leonarda; principally that she had been seen at a witches' Sabbath. Leonarda calmly denied all charges and, despite her lack of education, managed to dodge all Tissot's attempts to trick her, to put words in her mouth, to promise her leniency we all knew was a lie. That is, of course, allowed in cases of *crimen exceptum* such as witchcraft. The *Malleus* clearly states that prosecuting lawyers are permitted, indeed obliged, to use falsehoods and manipulations since we are playing the Devil at his own game in such cases.

The questioning went on for hours until the old lady could barely stand. The minutiae of her life were, for a while, interesting to me, as I had never known the minutiae of anyone's life other than my own. And we had much in common. I, too, know what it is like to go for days, even weeks, without speaking to a soul, to struggle for every meal and fear every winter.

But Leonarda gave the magistrate nothing, not even the suggestion that she might have cursed an ungenerous villager, and the crowd quickly grew restless. Even from my position close to the actors, I had to strain to hear what was happening since the crowd had resorted to conversations amongst themselves. The heavy doors were repeatedly opened and shut as people came and went, and the gavel was frequently hammered with shouts of, "Order, order!"

After each round of questioning, witness statements would be read. Things had indeed moved on since I had left the investigation in Tissot's hands—he had clearly interviewed all the accused in great detail. However, the women had not yet broken or denounced each other, other than Blaise, whose claims against Leonarda were outlandish, to say the least.

When Tissot had exhausted his questions several times over, the head Syndic stood and addressed the gallery. There had been no conference with the other three members of his panel because that part of the trial was a foregone conclusion. "Madame Leonarda Drouz has denied all the accusations against her. But, given the charges and the evidence therein, the investigation shall now proceed to a physical examination. I call upon the barber-surgeons Hans Frechez and Jean de Cortelles to shave Leonarda Drouz on every part of her body and inspect her for the marks of a witch. This, being in accordance with our laws and statutes, will take place in the adjoining chamber to preserve the dignity of the accused."

Groans of disappointment emanated from the crowd as they shuffled out, for everyone knew that that was where the real spectacle would begin. There would be very little dignity in what happened next, and I thanked God that I was a Small Council member and, therefore, eligible to attend.

That afternoon, I shuffled into the adjoining Small Chamber—which is, in all but name, a torture chamber—to take up a position for the shaving and witch-pricking. There was only standing room, so I bobbed and weaved to ensure my view was not blocked by others' hats, thanking God for my height. For, in truth, we were all bobbing and weaving and standing on our toes. Leonarda Drouz was brought in, had her clothes removed by two attending women, and was laid flat on a wooden table. Her body was white and sunken and disgusting, her empty breasts dropping to her waist like a goat's udders, her fragile bowlegs like sticks.

I so very much wanted to watch that total and complete possession and degradation of a woman's body. Everybody wanted to watch—I looked around the room and saw I was not the only one enthralled. There, I knew it! I am not perverted; all of us have these desires. All of us desire what is forbidden.

Since the disappearance of monasteries from Geneva and the current fashion for long beards like Calvin, the work of a barber-surgeon revolves almost entirely around high danger. No more delicate shaving of monks' tonsures, no more creative beard-shaping. Now, it is close proximity to either plague or witches and who can say which is worse? Accordingly, they are handsomely rewarded for their labors, and Frechez and de Cortelles wear their black robes lined with rich velvet and decorated with elaborate black lace far grander than the robes of councilmen such as myself, who fear Calvin's censures at any hint of ostentation. Frechez has been the teaching barber-surgeon at the Hospital de la Peste since its inception, and he is universally respected and feared, known as Le Serallion, or the cutter, although, in truth, he has no more training than a simple butcher. I thought briefly of Louise with her medical textbooks and studies with Paracelsus.

The barber-surgeons held their blades up to the light, then the shaving began. In their plague masks, they looked like two giant ravens pecking over her. I stiffened and felt the saliva keenly in my throat, embarrassed even to swallow, lest someone should hear. There was almost silence in the room; silence so I could hear every scrape of the blade and every whimper from Leonarda when they hurt her. For why should any delicacy be used on a witch? Silence because every one of us thirty men in the room was also watching intently and also perhaps embarrassed even to swallow.

Were they enthralled too? Surely, yes. Surely, we all have the same heart. The giant ravens began with her legs and then bade her sit up for her head. That was what everyone wanted to see, that delicious humiliation, almost too delicious to bear, and I am sure I heard moans of pleasure—or were they from me? —as the hair fell from her head, her scalp was revealed, and she became both less and more human. They examined her head with magnifying glasses, as they had done with every inch of her legs, regularly conferring with each other in hushed tones, their raven beaks clashing and nodding.

I only wished she were not old and haggard but young and fresh, for then there would be more pleasure in observing her degradation. The surgeons had saved her inner thighs for last, and they were meticulous there, going in close with their glasses. They were clearly looking for something in particular... Perhaps the witch's mark is often found in that area of the body. I was close enough to see the dark folds of her skin, and I wondered whether she smelled the same as Pernette, or different, worse.

They discussed her sex amongst themselves for a long time, and, after much conferring and muttering, they brought out a large instrument made of rusting iron—like a pair of tongs except with a large pear-shaped bulbous frame at its end. I could hardly believe something that large would go inside her. But then it was no larger, I suppose, than a baby's head. I saw her wince with pain as they inserted it, but she did not cry, and that surely was another sign of a witch.

I felt myself hardening and knew that the Devil was there, and I was glad for the distraction when someone cried, "She sheds no tears! It is the sorcery of silence!"

And there were mutters of, "Aye, aye, 'tis a witch for sure!" until Frechez raised his hands for calm.

"Wait, gentlemen. We will get to the pricking when it is time. There is still skin to examine for the Devil's mark."

They made her get on all fours and inserted the instrument first into one orifice, then the other. If she was a witch, perhaps that was not so unpleasant for her; indeed, do they not say that all women find pleasure in it? More conferring and nodding, then the surgeons paused to write extensive notes, leaving the instrument inside her.

It was eventually removed, with much blood and gore, and thrown with a clang into a silver tray while the surgeons reverentially took a wooden case, within which was an array of needles of different lengths. They inserted three—one into Leonarda's inner thigh, which caused her to erupt in screams, another into a brown mark on her arm, which also caused her to scream, and finally into a cluster of thick red marks on her elbow. At that, she made no sound, and the ravens bobbed and nodded as they scribbled copious notes to the chorus of, "Sorcery of silence, 'tis the Devil's mark there on her elbow for certain."

The prisoner was dressed and taken away, and the court adjourned for the day. I was relieved, for although I had battled against my crisis with the Devil during the ordeal, I was still suffering and needed to hobble home to battle him further. There is no doubt that the Devil was there in that chamber, harassing all good men.

❧

Back in the large courtroom the next morning, Tissot read from the barber-surgeons' report. "Gentlemen, I have here the report from the good barber-surgeons following their examination of Madame Leonarda Drouz. Madame Drouz has been found to have one mark of the Devil on her left elbow. She exhibited no pain, even when the largest pricking needle was inserted to a considerable depth. She also shed no tears during her shaving and examination—the sorcery of silence being another diabolical sign. We, therefore, conclude that there is strong evidence of collusion with the Devil and recommend that the court continue to move for Confession." Tissot paused for effect.

All eyes were on Drouz, dressed and with a bonnet covering her bald head, and there was fear in the room, for it seemed almost certain that she was a witch. However, during questioning, she continued the denials from the previous day. She claimed the mark on her elbow was a thick scar she had had since childhood.

"Since you continue to deny the accusations of witchcraft, in the face of considerable and mounting evidence, the court will move to use the strappado."

Then we were back in the Small Chamber; this time, huddled towards the corner of the room and the strappado frame, where the city executioner waited. Leonarda was made to kneel and clasp her hands together, and they were tied behind her with rope.

Tissot faced the audience as he addressed her. "Madame Leonarda Drouz, do you deny that you are a witch?"

For the first time, looking at the executioner and with an inkling of what lay ahead, she paused. "How can I say that I am a witch? I shall be condemned to Hell!"

Tissot nodded to the executioner. "Hoist her."

The executioner wound the rope until her body rose, her feet dragging only briefly since she was so light that she was quickly lifted into the air, the weight of her body taken by hanging shoulders. Surely, those old bones would shatter in no time; her skin was just a sheath for them.

As she hung there, Tissot asked again, "Do you deny that you are a witch?"

She made a desperate, breathy sound, but when he demanded that she repeat herself, she was silent.

"Speak up, madame!" Tissot shouted, nodding to the executioner, who waggled the rope to intensify her agony.

"Yes! I confess. I am a witch. Only let me down!" she cried. She was lowered, gently that time, onto her knees. Then the questions and answers flowed.

Tissot asked leading questions, of course, as he should, but her answers were so detailed, so specific, that they must have been true. "When did the Devil first appear to you?"

"Five years ago, just after my husband died."

"What form did he take?"

"The form of a bull."

"Did you copulate with him?"

"Yes."

"Describe this copulation so that the court may understand what vile acts the Devil makes women perform."

"He took me from behind, and his member was long and thin, and his semen was ice-cold."

So many women have mentioned this fact of the ice-cold demon seed, it must be true! Even if they only imagine it to have happened, a vision from the Devil is still evidence of witchcraft, according to many texts! Drouz went on to tell Tissot that she attended the Sabbath on three—no, four—occasions and that she saw all the other accused there.

"And who else did you see? You said there were many people at this Sabbath. Who else did you see from Satigny?"

Leonarda shook her head, exhausted and sobbing, so Tissot shouted, "Raise her again!" She was hoisted back up, and before she had a chance to speak, he shouted, "Add a weight!"

The executioner hung a weight from her foot, and a moment later, there was a dull crack. The crowd collectively winced as her shoulders were dislocated, and she screamed, though weakly.

"Who else was there?" Tissot roared up to her face.

She looked at him, then out at the crowd. Did she look at me? Did she smile as she cursed me? Cursed me with those words.

I knew exactly what she was going to say the moment before she said it.

"Louise de Peney."

My mouth went dry; I could not swallow. My ears burned, and I began to sweat profusely; my heart was beating so fast that I almost grasped at the person next to me for help. Yet I knew it. Everything was becoming clear and was as it should be.

"Speak up, woman! Which name did you give?"

"Louise de Peney. The wisewoman."

"Aha, a wisewoman." Tissot turned to the crowd. "And, as is so often the case, a wisewoman has been named."

The executioner released the rope gently again, and Leonarda was lowered to the floor, where she collapsed.

But she appeared energized by the new freedom of vindictiveness, and Tissot's questioning continued.

"Have you seen this Louise de Peney commit sorcerous acts?"

"Yes. It was she who delivered the devil child. Born in the caul, it was. And, ever since, the plague has been upon our village."

The room was alive with whispers. Clauda Rey was born in the caul, in that unnatural form, and it was Louise that brought her into the world. Everyone knows that a child born in the caul, like a Devil's egg festering inside its own foul fluid, is condemned to be a witch. Why did Louise allow that child to live?

❧ 14 ❧

SOLA SCRIPTURA

OCTOBER 7, 1545

Leonarda's testimony has dragged Louise into this case, and although it was shocking to hear those accusations—that she delivered a devil child, that she attended a Sabbath—there was a certain inevitability to it. Our paths are inextricably linked, mine and Louise's—I feel sure of it—and it is only a matter of time before they cross again. My head is full of feelings that I cannot define, and on Wednesday evening, hoping for some comfort and distraction, I attended Calvin's sermon at St. Peter's. With autumn fully upon us, there was a chill in the darkening air as people shuffled into the cavernous interior. The whole city—rich, middling, and poor, men, women, and children—all together to receive Calvin's instructions on how to live their lives. This is his vision: everyone working together, each knowing their place and responsibility. His teaching style is simple, without ostentation, so that even the most unlearned can understand.

The plague has become a major theme of his twice-weekly sermons. The practicalities, of course—the church is the main forum for explaining how to protect ourselves and others, how to prevent the spread. Rumors about plague-spreaders are either quelled or stoked, depending on the news, while supplications are made for plague workers, hospital visitors, grave diggers, and so on.

But Calvin also addresses the plague on a spiritual level. He reminds us of the gospel of Paul, St. Paul being Calvin's favorite mouthpiece by far. St. Paul bears witness that God had sent the plague on Corinth because the Holy Supper had not been so reverently treated there as it ought. Calvin thus blames the Catholic mass and its superstitions—the plague was God's punishment for dishonoring the true sacraments. Keeping to the new forms of worship is the best way of ensuring bodily and public health.

Given that the new Peney trials are the talk of the city, I had expected Calvin to address witchcraft, or at least heresy, in some way. Instead, he expounded on another of his favorite topics—the Psalms. The Psalms are at the heart of Calvin's teaching, and he labored to produce the Genevan psalter as a songbook of psalms even the lowliest worker or peasant can sing so that all can worship equally.

In this sermon, he told us, his eager flock, that he had begun work on commentaries on the Psalms, which would eventually become a book or series of books.

"I have been accustomed to call this book, I think not inappropriately, An Anatomy of All the Parts of the Soul, for there is no emotion of which anyone can be conscious that is not here represented as a mirror. Or rather, the Holy Spirit has here drawn to life all the griefs, sorrows, fears, doubts, hopes, cares, perplexities—in short, all the distracting emotions with which the minds of men are wont to be agitated."

I certainly felt—and feel—agitated. Because where in the Psalms are these emotions I feel? Where is the anxiety I feel at the thought of any human interaction? Where is the simultaneous love and hatred I feel for my solitude? Where is the constant need to fantasize, the arousal, the revulsion, the constant skirting of torture and humiliation around the edges of my mind, like the flames of Hell lapping on its shores? Where is all that mirrored in the Psalms? Either we are all lying to ourselves, and that is surely the worst blasphemy one could imagine, or it is me and me alone. I can only conclude that these feel ings are temptations of the Devil, implanted by God to test me, and therefore, ultimately noble and good.

Calvin continued. "Here, the prophets themselves lay open all their innermost thoughts and affections and then call upon each of us to do the same. We must examine ourselves in order that none of the many infirmities to which we are subject, nor the many vices with which we abound, may remain concealed. It is certainly a rare and singular advantage when all lurking places are discovered, and the heart is brought into the light, purged from that most baneful infection: hypocrisy."

The many vices with which we abound? Calvin says we are all, even he, tarnished with the contrary vices, but is he really tarnished with my vices? Are we all hypocrites? I can only hope that we are... Surely, we all think like me. But I also fear the possibility that we are all like me. Which is worse? I do not know.

"It is by perusing these inspired compositions," he concluded, "that men will be most effectually awakened to a sense of their maladies and, at the same time, instructed in seeking remedies for their cure."

If I were to be cured, how empty my life would be. Without my vices to think upon—and indeed that is all I do, I think upon them, I do not act. Therefore, I am not truly tarnished, and my outward actions are all in the service of God, so the balance in my soul favors the good, I am sure of it. Then may I never be cured! Let my heart never be brought into the light! How could I ever lay open my inmost thoughts and affections? Let my particular infirmities fester like the delicious wounds they are. I shall never give them up.

The congregation shuffled out into the cool night, and I was amongst them, on my guard against any that might be afflicted, as always. I held a pomander to my nose and kept my head down, but my height makes it very difficult to be hidden in a crowd. Should someone be looking out for me, of course. And someone was.

"Henry!" Calvin pushed his way down the aisle, waving a book of Psalms above his head to attract my attention. Fending off well-wishers and acolytes waiting to speak to him, he reached me. "I thought I saw you. Excellent. How are you?"

"Quite well, thank you."

"Good, good. Now listen, I'd like you to come to dinner this evening. I have a surprise for you." My terror must have shown because he laughed and said, "I can see you don't like surprises. Very well, I shall tell you. I have invited Antoine Froment and Marie Dentière to dine with me, and, to my mild astonishment, I must confess, they have accepted. As you know, we have not been on the best of terms in recent years, but with him preaching informally all over the place, I wish to bring him back into the fold, as it were. There may be a position for him at the hospital if he would consider giving up that ridiculous shop of his."

The terror I felt had changed to horror, and I hoped it didn't show. I did not want to dine with Calvin and submit to the anxiety of thinking about what to say to the cleverest man in all Christendom for a whole evening. But to add two people from whom I had been hiding since childhood to the mix... I tried to smile.

Calvin kindly placed a hand on my arm. "So, you will come. I thought you might be able to help me rebuild some bridges. I would invite you to walk home with me now, except that I have to stop at the consistory to collect some papers and confer with a colleague. But you are welcome to go to my house directly, and Idelette will take care of you. Don't look so worried, man! This is an excellent prospect for you. And since you don't have parents of your own to take care of your marriage—they have daughters, you know." He winked as he turned to leave.

I realized I had not spoken other than, "Quite well, thank you." What on earth do people say? The more time I spend with people, the more I regret all those years alone.

I watched him leave, then dashed around the corner as I felt my mouth fill with saliva, bile rising from my stomach, and that dull sense of dread I last felt when I had eaten a poorly cooked chicken that made me ill.

I leaned over the low wall at the side of the cathedral and vomited up everything I had eaten that day. The violence of the human body is always a shock, with its primitive and involuntary urges.

I wiped my mouth but could still smell that sickly smell of vomit, and when I walked close to the nearest street torch, I saw with dismay that my robes had not quite escaped the splatter. What foulness lies within us, just waiting to emerge from every orifice? There was nothing for it; I would have to go home, change into my other robe and stockings, and wipe my shoes. As I marched up the hill towards rue Tabazan, my mind worked frantically on possible excuses and escapes, but I had none. My career depended on my attendance.

I had told different things to Calvin, to Froment, to Dentière, to myself. They would all ask the same question: why did I choose to live alone? Sometimes I ask myself the same question when I could have had a family. But I did not deserve a new family, with my true family so cruelly taken and I spared. And I was only a child when I told the first lie. I think sometimes we become so entangled in our lies, so involved in our fantasies, that we lose sight of what is real. We lose the ability to judge what is right.

I was in such a rush that I was forced to hasten my door handle ritual, conducting the wiping, counting, re-wiping, and prayer at a much faster pace than usual. No, it would not do. After I entered the house, I left again, looking about furtively, and I re-enacted the ritual just to be sure. It cannot be rushed. It is not superstition; it is a matter of basic hygiene. And I cursed all three of them—Calvin, Froment, and Dentière—for disrupting my precious routine.

By the time I had changed, conducted the closing and locking ritual, and set off back to Calvin's house, I was in such a state of agitation that I could barely contain my heart rate, and, despite the cold evening, I was sweating through my shirt to my doublet, which I feared would be stained. It was a cold, unpleasant sweat. I would have to clean two sets of clothes.

I hardly like to imagine how late I was when I knocked on the door.

Idelette opened it with raised eyebrows and a flustered expression, but, fortunately, it was not me with whom she was irritated. "He springs these guests on me unannounced. I have to go back and supervise the cook. You just go on through; you'll find them in the parlor."

I walked further into the house than the last time when I had been in his street-facing office. I heard Calvin's voice as I went down the dim corridor toward the back room.

"He is a strange fellow. Very clever and an excellent worker for the council. Never makes a mistake when he writes. But he hardly speaks. Looks at you as if he hasn't heard or understood a word. And, when he does speak, it comes out as an apology. Makes you feel distinctly uncomfortable, I must say."

"Twenty-nine, you say? How did he get the council position at such a young age?"

"Ah well, a remnant of the old ways of doing things—his father died while in office, so he was permitted to stand for the position. That is all changing, of course. But I'm sure he'll be adequate to the task."

I wondered naively if they could be talking about someone else until a woman's voice confirmed that it was me.

"Ah yes, now I remember him very well. How odd that he told you he was living with us? I am sure I offered to take him in, but he refused, saying he had a place at the orphanage."

"How strange. I imagine he was ashamed to tell me he came from the orphanage. Perhaps we should not press him on it. In any case, he takes everything literally, which means he does exactly what I say. A perfect protégé, I would say."

The woman laughed. "Sounds like a perfect husband too!"

Perhaps I should have knocked or announced my presence some other way because when I slid into the room, they stopped talking abruptly, startled at my interruption. I felt hotter than ever as I was confronted with two people who had shown me such kindness yet which I hadn't seen in more than ten years. Froment and Marie rose to greet me, Calvin remaining in his chair, smiling and watching our reunion with interest.

They were as handsome a couple as they had been before. He was dressed in simple, black, and fur-lined robes like Calvin, but with a soft, feathered cloth cap instead of Calvin's severe, skull-fitting one. She wore a black dress, close-fitting with a corset and modern farthingale, yet demure and with a neat white bonnet.

She beamed and moved forward to take my hands.

I fought my natural urge to resist touch and allowed her.

"Henry! Is it really you?"

My eyes suddenly swam. There was a time when I imagined her as my mother and loathed and punished myself for my disloyalty. Did I squander my chance?

"The last time I saw you was in Antoine's schoolroom—oh, it must have been twelve or thirteen years ago."

Froment then took his turn to greet me with both hands.

"Henry! I had thought you long dead of plague and mourned whenever I thought of you until I saw your name appear in the new magistrates list this year! I voted for you, of course. In fact, I wrote to you just after your election, in early March, it would have been. Did you not receive it?"

"I did not, I'm afraid." I lied, for the letter is in the chest under the floorboards. I had read it perhaps a hundred times before deciding not to respond.

"How strange... I had it delivered to the council office in your name. Well, no matter. It is wonderful to see you now."

"And how tall and handsome."

They both beamed at me—Calvin too—and I felt like a child.

I took so long to concoct a response that Froment moved to save me, and we both spoke at the same time.

"Where do you—"

"I— Sorry, go on," he said, laughing.

"Where do you live?" Good God, is that the best I could do? With everything he taught me? Everything I have read? How I loathe myself.

"We have lived out in Thonon these past ten years. I am a shopkeeper now, Henry. I enjoy it very much."

Calvin interjected as he rose from his armchair to lead us to the dinner table. "And now you can preach twice over—from the pulpit and in your apron."

Froment smiled. "It is indeed the priesthood of all believers."

"And perhaps we shall discuss over dinner where we women fit into this priesthood, John," said Marie.

So boldly did she play with him!

We ate in the kitchen, Idelette serving us soup and wine before sitting to my right, with the married couple opposite us and Calvin at the head of the table.

"Now, tell us, Henry," said Marie as we broke bread, "Calvin says you are working for him on this witchcraft case."

I had just taken a mouthful of bread and chewed awkwardly while nodding as the beginning of my response. "It is my honor to serve Calvin and the city as an investigator to the witchcraft accusations in Satigny. The trials are now ongoing." I thought of Louise, languishing in her cell. Perhaps she was thinking of me too.

"There can hardly be anyone left in Satigny," said Froment. "Is that your plan, Calvin, to wipe the place out completely? Then how would we get our wine? I don't know, this witchcraft business. I feel as if we are being doubly tricked—I believe there's nothing that makes the Devil happier than seeing these rollicking witch trials, with every neighbor turning on one another."

Calvin shook his head and wagged his finger. "These are not light-hearted matters, Antoine. We are under attack from Satan, and we must fit ourselves with the full armor of God."

"You are right. There is heresy and evil temptation everywhere. But what I mean is that the fortress is not Geneva, with its high walls and cannons protecting us against these pathetic women—they can't all be guilty. The fortress must be in our own minds, against the Devil's attacks on souls."

"Are you saying, Froment, that witchcraft is not heresy? Surely there is no greater heresy."

"Do you deny, Calvin, that he who lusts after his neighbor's wife has committed adultery?"

"I do not deny it; it is the case. Lust is a sin."

"Do you deny that he who still believes the Mass to be a true sacrifice for the quick and the dead is an idolator?"

"I do not deny it; you know he who believes in the Catholic Mass is an idolator."

"Then I say that he who ascribes the power of witchcraft to a mere woman is, in their heart, a blasphemer because this power belongs to God only. If they can destroy crops, bring plague and storms, and fly through the air, then we should worship them as gods. If more ridiculous or abominable crimes could have been invented, these poor women would have been charged with them. When, in reality, their only crimes are to be old, or poor, or—"

"And I thought," agreed Marie, "we no longer believed in miracles! These are miracles and, therefore, heresy! Do you not see the contradiction, Monsieur Calvin? The double standard and the triple standard?"

I also saw a double standard, as they debated such highly important matters in such a flippant way, darting from this statement to that in between laughter and sips of wine.

Calvin said, "Look, we have to be pragmatic. You know, and I know, that not all of these women are witches. But the crime of witchcraft is lèse-majesté—against God—and the wrath of God will be brought down on anyone who refuses to prosecute it. It is treason. And it is better that a few unfortunate innocents should burn than that a single witch goes unpunished. This is what I told Henry here."

Marie sighed, then looked at me. "I hear that the new suspect named today is Louise de Peney."

I choked on my food a little. "You know her?"

As soon as I had spoken, I remembered Louise had told me she and Marie were former colleagues. All the better, I had not revealed my acquaintance with a suspected witch.

"Of course, Henry! We were Sisters together before I saw the light! She was just a child then, of course. After I left, I visited the Poor Clares many times in the early 1530s, trying to persuade them. Poor stubborn creatures! I have only limited sympathy for them—I tried very hard, you know. If only they knew how good it is to be with a handsome husband." She put her hand on Froment's arm, fond. "And how agreeable it is to God. I lived for such a long time in that darkness and hypocrisy, but thanks be to God, I came to the true light of truth. And now, I have five beautiful children."

Calvin smiled. "So, you see, Antoine, there is little compassion to be had for these women, who have squandered their chances. By allowing the Devil in, they have brought this on themselves."

Froment said, "But perhaps there are those who wish to direct all their love towards God, rather than towards Earthly things."

Dentière placed her hand on his arm again. "I say never shall a man attain the perfect love of God, who has not loved to perfection some creature in this world."

"So, you agree then, Marie," asked Calvin, "that a woman's place is in the home? And that the purpose of a woman's education is domesticity?"

"You cannot trick me, Monsieur Calvin. We argued back and forth on this many times. Undoubtedly, we agree a woman's place is in the home. But must we be silent in our homes? What is the point of teaching us the scriptures if we are to be silent about them?"

"The point is to educate your children—"

"So that they can be silent, too? Come now, Calvin, you married an Anabaptist, after all. Anabaptist women are preachers just like men. What say you, Idelette?"

Idelette spoke quietly. "Well, I am not an Anabaptist anymore..." She concentrated on her soup, eyes low.

Marie sighed and rolled her eyes. She looked at me then, and I was very conscious that it must surely have been my turn to speak, but, fortunately, she did not seem to require it of me. "In 1536, a work was written, The War and Deliverance of the City of Geneva. It was published as a pamphlet, and lauded, and preached. In 1539, A Very Useful Letter was published, calling for very much the same thing. The adoption of the Reformation, the support of Calvin and Farel, the importance of educating women, and of expelling the Catholic clergy from France. Two works, both well-written, both in perfect French, both with the same arguments. But the second was buried, suppressed, banned. Why? What was the difference?"

Calvin said, "But the War and Deliverance was written by... why, it was written by you, Antoine, was it not?"

Antoine and Marie spoke at the same time, laughing.

"My wife wrote it!"

"I wrote it!" Marie smiled. "That is the difference. I wrote them both! My first was anonymous; my second was written as myself. I do not believe this city would publish anything by a woman author now."

"Then you have ruined it for everybody, my dear."

I was both elated and intimidated by the lofty discussions on display. Their arguments brought in Greek philosophers, Rabelais, the

Church fathers... Such leaps of logic, such eloquence of thought, and I had read everything they quoted and followed it all. As I write this now, I imagine the ripostes I could have given. I could have reminded Marie Dentière of the seriousness of the issue, as she so flippantly talked of women and witchcraft as if it were nothing but a parlor game of rhetoric. That would have put her in her place. I could have questioned Antoine, who seemed to deny that witches exist at all. What would that mean for our investigation? Well, it is heresy enough that women believe themselves capable of witchcraft, and that is sufficient justification for punishing them.

I often wanted to contribute something, but by the time I had constructed a sentence, the moment had always passed.

DE PRAESTIGIIS DAEMONUM

OCTOBER 8, 1545

In the morning, Leonarda Drouz was questioned for the final time. It is customary to ask the prisoner to confirm their confession the day following torture to ensure it was not a lie extracted under duress.

"Madame Leonarda Drouz, do you confirm with heart and mouth everything that you confessed yesterday? Or do you wish to undergo the strappado again?"

Leonarda was standing, but barely. Her useless arms hung limp at her sides, so she had to use her belly to lean against the stand, unable to stay upright unaided. "I stand by my confession. No more strappado."

Her full confession was read out—the confession that would send her to her death and that accused Louise of attending a Sabbath and bringing forth a Devil's child.

How easy it is to put words in people's mouths. How easy it is to re-invent a story. The other trials unfolded as the first had, as these trials always do. I watched them all, both dreading and hoping for the mention of Louise. For if she were implicated, it could be my chance to possess her and maybe to save her.

Blaise Besson broke the most easily, as expected—indeed, she had denounced herself and the other women already. It is hardly necessary to describe the grotesque spectacle of her shaving and pricking; suffice to recount that the sight of her disease-ridden body drew horrified, satisfied gasps from the crowd and provided a warning to all of the dangers of extra-marital relations. No strappado was required for her since she was more than willing to comply with Tissot. She cackled and yelled curses at the crowd, wild-eyed, which drew more delighted gasps. Long after she could have been taken down, Tissot kept her on the stand; he demanded more details of her dalliances with the Devil, and she regaled him with increasingly outlandish and obscene tales of her demonic sexual encounters. It was as if they were performing a play: he, with pre-rehearsed lines, and her, improvising on the spot. She was eventually dragged away to a chorus of cheers. Blaise did not mention Louise, but since Leonarda Drouz had struck the tinder, the flame of Louise's demise was lit.

Jeanne Valleron was next, and I feared for the barber-surgeons as they examined her, going so close to the body of a plague-spreader. After much exploring of flesh and pricking and screaming and nodding of beaked masks, they were unable to ascertain whether or not she bore the Devil's mark, so they moved on to the questioning. I must say that the process of repeated torture is particularly effective in extracting full confessions. Madame Valleron began her trial, claiming to be an innocent plague-worker who had toiled her whole life to help rid Calvin's godly city of pestilence. But after one round of the strappado, she admitted the truth—that the Devil had appeared to her, in the garden, in the form of a toad. He had made her swear allegiance to him, and yes, she thought that perhaps she did perform the osculum infame—it may have been only in a dream, but no matter.

"And did you ride with the Devil, Madame?" roared Tissot into her ear as she knelt, her broken shoulders hanging limp, clasped hands still attached to the rope as the executioner stood ready to hoist her again should she fail to reply. She nodded emphatically.

"And what did you say to the Devil on this ride?"

Madame Valleron was confused, shaking her head and looking up at

Tissot with desperate eyes. So, he prompted her. "Something about a stick, perhaps?"

"Oh yes!" She nodded, relieved. "I said, 'White stick, black stick, carry me where you will go. Go, in the Devil's name, go!"

Exactly the same words as Blaise Besson told me back in Satigny prison—so it must be true!

After a second round of the strappado, Valleron had named not only Louise but all manner of other women from the village. Fiendish beings are multiplying there like worms in a garden.

As the prosecutor twisted and turned them, the women seemed to remember more, their narratives fleshing out with detail and corroborating each other. Subliminal hints became facts, fragments of ideas, and petty jealousies molded themselves into stories. There was so much confusion between remembrances and imaginings that any difference between the two became blurred for the women—for all of us in the courtroom. And in truth, what is the difference between the two when it is known that the Devil also appears to us in dreams? I began to see everything differently, to rewrite the story of Satigny for myself.

Yes, six years ago, Louise de Peney gave the wife of Jean Grippo, who was great with child, a special drink, whereupon the child was born dead. Around the same time, she touched the body of Henriette Moget with a green salve, whereupon poor Henriette grew ill and still languishes in sickness today. Five years ago, she prepared an unguent for George Melliez's stomach complaint, and soon thereafter, both his cow and his goat died. She had obtained the unguent from the Devil himself at the Sabbath. Her singing was known to enchant wild beasts and turn the minds of men to lustful thoughts. Three times, Louise de Peney had been seen flying through the sky with the Devil.

Indeed, Louise was responsible for every stillborn child and every mother dead in childbed since she arrived in Satigny. Why? So she could dig up their graves and offer their unbaptized souls to Satan for his army. Gasps of horror from the gallery. All those things were, of course, possible since she was present at all those events. Louise de Peney was frequently seen with squirrels, and, being her familiars, they showed no fear and rode on her shoulder, which is against the laws of nature. This, too, could not be denied.

It appeared Louise was also responsible for adverse weather events. Four years ago, she brought the hailstorm that destroyed the harvest that year. And all while her garden remained plentiful; this is known because, in her gloating triumph, she shared her fruit and vegetables with the village. She has been seen to go out in lightning storms; this is known because she attended the birth of Coline Gay's daughter in Choully, even though the weather would have terrified any mere mortal into staying indoors. I smiled as I imagined her battling through rain and wind to reach a patient in need; of course, she would.

Especially if she knew herself to be under the Devil's protection—could it be possible?

The most damning evidence against Louise came from Claudine Rey. Still beautiful after shaving and pricking and time spent in a filthy prison, she began the questioning with her head held high, dignified and defiant. But Tissot's methods helped her to see that, yes, her child born in the caul was indeed a demon. She described how Louise brought a clear sack from between her legs. Like a monstrous bubble, which Louise then popped, allowing its foul waters to spread their pestilence into the village, where they would fester for the next ten years. And what was left was a tangle of malformed limbs with a head attached, and Louise did not smother it there and then but tapped it until it breathed and taught Clauda to feed and love the thing. A monstrous perversion of a mother's love! Perhaps Louise truly was in league with the Evil One.

Five women, five trials, five spectacles. Or rather, four spectacles because little Clauda Rey could not talk and therefore could not be questioned, and there was no need for the barber-surgeons to prick a body that amounted to one whole Devil's mark. The sentencing took place on a Friday, all five together. The sentence was as expected. Two of the women wept. Blaise laughed, and so Clauda laughed too, either because her malformed brain did not understand or because she was ready to meet her master in Hell. And either of these reasons is a vindication of all that is being done.

There are gallows in several places around the city, but most executions, and certainly all the most important executions, take place on Champel Hill at Plainpalais. Indeed, when the suburbs were destroyed in 1536, the only piece of architecture to survive at Champel was the gallows. It is only a few minutes' walk from the hospital, but outside the city walls. On execution days, the city gates are opened, and all citizens able to are expected to attend. Apart from Calvin and the other city fathers, of course, who do not require the moral education. As the masses walk towards the Field of Execution, as it is known, the hilltop gallows are always visible on the horizon, a reminder of God's justice.

That day, there were five nooses waiting on the horizon, and I noticed—with a lurch in my stomach—that one hung longer than the others to reach Clauda's lower neck. Good God, surely, they were not going to hang the little girl as well? But of course, they were; she is a witch—I had just never seen it done.

But I have seen many executions, of course, so I pushed through the crowd to find a place to stand, weaving between people selling snacks, flags, and other sundries. I imagined many Satigny villagers would be there and, sure enough, found myself next to Donzel. We nodded at each other as the crowd parted for the cart carrying the prisoners from the Bourg-du-Four, led by the lieutenant. The women were not bound that day, and all of them held hands as they were ushered onto the platform. But it was too late for this female solidarity. They had condemned themselves and each other long ago.

"A job well done, Magistrate," Donzel said as he nudged my shoulder in that way I found so irritating. He spoke through a mouthful of pie that he had bought from one of the many vendors taking advantage of the event.

"Quite."

The little girl was screaming, and it was an unbearable, unearthly sound. A sound from the Devil indeed.

"Why did the women not smother the child themselves last night?" I asked.

"Ah, they are always watched. It's a common thing to attempt, but that would spoil the whole show, wouldn't it? And since Calvin banned theater, this is the only entertainment we've got."

As the nooses were placed around their necks, one by one, I looked behind me and saw Madame Folliez in the crowd. I tried to avoid her gaze, but too late—our eyes met. I could not read her expression, but she must have been satisfied to see justice done, even if her own lying-in maid had escaped. We had both acted as we should.

The lieutenant made his speech, but it was hard to hear above Clauda's screaming, and shortly after, the executioner pulled the platform away in one smooth movement. With a crack, all five necks broke at once. The crowd erupted into cheers and jeers, riding on a wave of power that was beyond all of us. Praise God that our new executioner has such expertise, for in the past, I have seen long, drawn-out hangings where the prisoner writhed for a full ten minutes. I have seen heads turn bright blue and globular before they died.

As the women's bodies fought their final involuntary death throes, I felt I should say something to Donzel. It was odd to stand there watching and waiting for their legs to go still as he calmly devoured his pie. "I saw you, *châtelain*. In the forest on Sabbath night two weeks back. I saw what happened."

Donzel stopped eating, his mouth wide open, but did not take his eyes away from the gallows. After a measured pause, he said, "I am not the only one who has been seen in places he should not be, magistrate. Or, rather, with people he should not be with. It is not like the city, where you can lose yourself in the crowd. The fields of Satigny are wide open, and we don't have many distractions. When you go out riding, you are seen. When you commune with wisewomen, you are seen. And people think...what they want to think."

"I don't know what you are referring to, but—"

"Louise de Peney is a witch. And you are supposed to be a witch hunter. Not a witch's suitor."

A witch hunter. A suitor! How do I feel about those titles? In truth, I do not know.

Well and truly dead, the bodies were lowered and transferred to the adjacent pyre. That took some time, and I moved away from Donzel and away from Madame Folliez as close to the pyre as I could manage, close enough that I could smell the sulfur that had been sprinkled on the wood pile. I kept a pomander held to my nose and my eyes low or on the pyre, lest I see anyone else from the village.

Then I was warmed by the flames, and as the bodies began to melt, the faces liquefying into grotesque shapes, I began to stiffen again. The smell of roasting meat mingled with sulfur filled the air. The scent of it, along with the sight of the charred, crumbling corpses, caused me to reach my moment of crisis. Nobody would have noticed my slight convulsion, with all eyes fixed on the fire. I gasped as it was then, in that crescendo of horror, that I had the revelation. I knew that Louise was not a witch. She was not like those women who had sold her. And I would save her. As the bodies blackened, melted, charred, and crumbled, I stood as impassive as I could and tried not to smile because a beautiful plan was formulating itself.

Thanks be to God that He revealed himself to me in that way, and I knew then what I must do: I had to go to Louise, and that evening, before they came to arrest her. I would not hesitate this time—I would ask her for her hand, with no fear of refusal because the alternative was her death. I would be her savior, restored in her estimation. The balance would be redressed. Of course, it was a great shame we would not be able to live in her house, but since her property would fall to me as her husband and I have been convicted of nothing, I would sell it and my own, and we could live comfortably in exile. Who does not live in exile these days? Geneva itself is a city of refugees; there is no shame in it.

His will be done in all things.

I did not stay until the end of the execution; I pushed through the crowds and raced back to rue Tabazan to collect essential items— clothing, pomanders, and as much money as I could carry from my chest. I took my diary but left the Malleus. Those days were over. The bag weighed heavily on my shoulder as I lurched over to the city livery, where I planned to demand a horse on magistrate business. But there was no one there—the whole city was at the Field of Execution, and no doubt many of the residents would be proceeding directly to taverns to continue the celebration.

I agonized for a short time. There was no way I could walk to Satigny with that heavy bag—it would take me all night. And we would need a horse for our escape. There were ten in the stalls, noses in bags of straw, and it would take nothing for me to vault the gate, open it from the other side, and release one. In fact, I could see that the trusty steed I had been using was there. If anyone saw me, I could say I intended to pay and threaten to inform the Small Council that the city livery had been left unmanned. I am no stranger to theft, and it was theft in the name of God. I took my horse—the old one, what luck! Within five minutes, I was at the city gates, and, to my delight, they were also unmanned. This was truly God's will. And yet, how we have left ourselves open to attack from the Savoyards, with the whole city at this witch-burning!

The smell of burned wood almost overpowered the smell of burned flesh; as I crossed the fields towards the Pont D'Arve, I could see the smoke from the pyre—a column of black rising into the blazing sky. Would I miss this city where I had lived in hiding and silence my whole life? The journey passed in a blur of vague plans... Did it really matter? Louise would know where to go. We could go to Annecy, as she had been told to time and time again. We could be there within two days. Or we could head further—towards the west of France or even the Holy Land. A pilgrimage. There was still at least a month before the first snow.

The sky was a blaze of color. The Jura themselves seemed to glow. I passed all the places where we had had our encounters. The Nant d'Avril running through the pretty wood where I had first seen her, and she had stood above me like an angel. The glorious junction of rivers that she had revealed to me like the secrets of Heaven. And the road into the village where she had come running to beg at my feet. By the time I approached Louise's house, my heart was racing; I could barely keep the smile from my face, and when do I ever smile?

But there was somebody there already. Someone had gotten there before me. I knew before I heard the voices, and I knew who was there before I saw him. It was almost dark, and I had not been seen. How had the news traveled that fast? I had left the city when the execution crowd had barely dispersed. He must have been there too and raced back before me.

Bernard was standing in Louise's front garden. They were facing each other, and—God forbid—they were holding hands. He was shaking hers in a beseeching, urgent manner, and she was—thank God —shaking her head.

And then, she began to nod. And then they embraced. How can I describe my feelings? Heartbreak? Perhaps. I was numb for a moment, in denial, although I should have known, I should have known, I should have moved sooner. And then the blue sky of my imagined future was obscured by rolling black storm clouds of jealous rage.

They were looking around as if afraid of being seen, and I was damned if those traitors would see me, so I stole away quickly, denying myself a last glance back. I raced to Geneva as the sky darkened and the world collapsed around me.

And yes, how easy it is to re-invent a story. To tell a different story. Only a few minutes before, I had been reminiscing about our encounters in the forest—the squirrels, the kindness she showed me with her cures, the honesty with which she spoke about her knowledge of the stars and of medicine, the moment she touched my wrist.

Now, I see all these things differently. The squirrels are her spirit animals, the knowledge of the stars her heresy. The touching on the wrist: "The judges and assessors must not allow themselves to be touched physically by the witch... Her hands are as bands for binding, for when they place their hands on a creature to bewitch it, then with the help of the Devil, they perform their design." And the sleeping cure she wanted to give me—of course, now I see everything clearly, for the *Malleus* explains how witches can stop men from performing. "When the member is stirred and becomes erect but yet cannot perform, it is a sign of witchcraft!" It is true that I never could succeed when I tried to use her in my fantasies. She must have touched my clothing with her potion at some moment. And then her obsession with the stars: "But devils are subservient to certain influences of the stars because magicians observe the course of certain ones to evoke the devils." I was lucky she had not gone further.

I must move quickly before she does indeed go further. Louise de

Peney is a witch, after all. The village has protected her for too long. And now she will be made to feel the blade of her own sword.

The *Malleus* was right. "All wickedness is but little to the wickedness of a woman," and "they can turn the minds of men to inordinate love or hatred." She has turned me to hatred.

❧ 16 ❧

SI FALLOR, SUM

OCTOBER 16, 1545

In the morning, Louise de Peney was arrested. The guards had set out from the city before dawn. Even if I had wanted to stop it, I could not; the evidence against her was too great. And indeed, I had much more to add to the women's testimonies.

It was reported that a crowd gathered around her cottage before she emerged, a silent crowd comprising much of the village. It was reported that Bernard made a scene, shouting, "Is there no one who will speak for this woman?" until he was dragged away on pain of imprisonment. Apparently, when they knocked on her door and called her name, there was a long pause. Then she opened it calmly, already dressed in her cloak, and closed the door behind her. She held out her hands to be tied.

"Such beauty, such bravery, such dignity, sir!" said the boy I had sent to report back to me as he stood on my doorstep, catching his breath. "She could bewitch anybody!"

I smiled and looked across at the city prison, where she would be arriving on a cart. I would hide myself indoors before then, lest she saw me. It was not the time. Yes, my Louise, such dignity, of course. And we would be living side by side again, just like when we were young. Each in our own prison, but no matter.

I was able to make myself useful again then. It was necessary to search her house, and I volunteered for the role—an appropriate one for a junior magistrate. Certainly, a more appropriate role than the one I had previously been assigned.

With two apprentices to assist, I returned to Satigny yet again the following day. The journey had become familiar, and each time I had made it with a different attitude, consumed by different thoughts. My heart was heavy, yet perhaps less so than when I had stolen back to Geneva two nights before—stolen back to my house, unboarded the front door, quickly made a fire in the hearth, and burned the note I had written to the bailiffs I knew would have come. Hoping that no one had noticed my hasty departure—the permanent departure that had lasted only a few hours. Knowing in my heart that no one had noticed. No one ever noticed.

At first, I had despaired, for I knew I had lost Louise forever. But now, I have a strange sense of possessing her again, and it gives me some comfort. Since she languishes in the prison underneath the cathedral, she is only steps from my house. As a magistrate, I could manufacture a reason to visit her whenever I wanted. Not that I will, at least not yet. When that moment happens, it has to be of the greatest significance, and I need time to consider my speech. She must know the enormity of what she had lost. So, I have a sense of a new beginning. There is a new dynamic between us, two rivers flowing alongside each other, like the Arve and the Rhone at Junction. At some junction, one day, our rivers will join.

The apprentices and I entered the house that, only two days before, I had planned to inherit myself. I smiled at the thought that I might, in fact, still inherit it. A witch's property is not bequeathed to her family but reverts to the state. And perhaps Calvin might reward me for my efforts in the village. Another way to possess her, I suppose.

I assigned the young apprentices a pointless and long-winded task that would occupy them in the garden, wanting to be alone to explore the house. I moved through it slowly, revisiting the sitting room where we had stood together next to the bookcase. Some of those books could definitely be taken as evidence of heresy. The works of Paracelsus, undoubtedly. I climbed the creaking wooden staircase to the upper level. The house was in need of repair, and the upstairs landing listed precariously under my weight. I stooped to enter her bedroom. I could see where she slept—a simple cot with a wooden crucifix mounted on the wall above it. In a drawer next to her bedside, a set of carved wooden rosary beads. More evidence of heresy.

Her neatly-folded nightgown hung over the back of a wooden chair, the only other piece of furniture in the room. I could see the apprentices busy with their task in the garden, so I moved out of sight of the window, took the gown, and breathed in its scent. It smelled of lemon and herbs and warmth. It smelled of her.

The extended kitchen, which took up the whole back of the house, would be our most important site for evidence. I had already seen her distillation equipment since she had not hidden it from me, and there it was, all on display. A myriad of every-sized glass bottles, linked by tubing of various materials—wood, glass, hide. But the most clinching piece of evidence turned out to be her notebooks. Filled with her neat handwriting, interspersed with illustrations, maps, and diagrams that I could not always decipher. They looked like spells.

Then there was the most damning evidence of all. A Study on the Possibility of Preventing Plague in the General Population by Way of Small Exposure.

This was nothing other than plague-spreading. She had mentioned something about Paracelsus's early efforts at—what had she called it— inoculation? Perhaps her intentions were good, perhaps not. Who is to say that the intentions of the plague-spreaders who killed my family were not good—from their perspective? Perhaps my father had done them wrong. If she is one of them, if she is a plague-spreader, it will be much easier for me.

OSCULUM INFAME

OCTOBER 23, 1545

I met with Tissot in his office at the City Hall to submit my evidence. I stood in front of his desk while he leafed through my notes, occasionally nodding and smiling to himself, making his own.

"I must say this is an impressive body of evidence you have collected here, magistrate. I must congratulate you on a very thorough preparation of this case. You have made my job very easy. You will, naturally, present all this on the stand in due course... We will make an excellent show of this, shall we not? You'll have to speak up, of course, though—your voice is far too quiet."

I coughed. "I would like to request that I not take the stand, sir."

There was a pause before he looked up, incredulous, as if he had misheard. "Are you mad? The witness statements are crucial! The syndics will expect it! The crowd will expect it!"

I stood impassive, coughing again, and focused on the wall behind him. "If I may refer you, sir, to Part Three, Chapter 32 of the *Malleus Maleficarum*, which states that the judge 'is not bound either to publish the names of the deponents or bring them before the accused, unless they themselves should freely and willingly offer to come before the accused and lay their depositions in her presence.'"

He sighed. "I can see Calvin chose you for your thoroughness, if not your pedantry. What reason do you give for not wanting to take the stand?"

"As stated in the *Malleus*, it is by reason of the danger incurred by the deponents that the judge is not bound to do this."

"Danger? You fear that the accused will cause you harm?"

"Yes. Precisely."

"Very well." He sighed, crossing something out on his paper. "In truth, the evidence against this woman is so strong that our case will not suffer for any lack of public depositions."

"If she is found not guilty, what will happen?"

He looked at me, amused. "That is very unlikely. Why do you ask?"

"Well, she may not confess."

"They all confess eventually. And, even if—by some miracle—she holds out, as I said, the evidence you have collected against her speaks for itself. Congratulations on a very thorough case. Watch and learn from the next stages, and you'll be conducting these yourself in no time."

❦

Tissot is known for his meticulousness, so it was to be some time before the case went to trial. He would also have to fend off attacks from the other senior prosecutors—there is always an internal struggle for control of the biggest cases. Autumn is truly upon us now; it has rained solidly for a week, and I spend most of my time looking out of the window.

My anger has dissipated, and I feel that I have her in my possession, so close. My main preoccupation has been the consideration of whether or not to visit her. I am sure she is waiting for me to, and I am surprised she has not asked for me already.

Now she is in the main Geneva prison, which lies under the cathedral—only a few steps from my house and only a few steps from the convent. All those years, we lived so close, unbeknownst to each other, and now we are together again. Of course, now she is cloistered even more than before, yet she feels closer somehow.

I spend a lot of time at the window where I had spent so much of my childhood. From my vantage point, I can see the entrance to the prison and all the comings and goings. I try to manufacture a reason for visiting, but I do not have one. So, I watch and wait and hope she will request to speak with me. Surely, that is what she is thinking. Yes, she has probably not been given the right. She has probably asked and been refused.

Eventually, I decided to write her a letter. Why did I not think of this before? I spent a day or so composing it in my head so that, by the time I sat down to write, I knew almost precisely what I wanted to say, and the words flowed easily. At first, I wrote several pages, but each time I reread my work, I felt more and more ashamed, so the final letter was just one paragraph. I am quite pleased with my composition, and I believe that I have captured the correct tone.

Dear Louise,

I trust that you are well. I waited to see if you would send for me, but I imagine you are not permitted visitors. I would like you to know that I forgive you. I would also like you to know that I have faith in you and in God's justice. Our souls being intertwined, I believe that all will be for the best.

Your humble servant in the Lord,

Henry Aubert

I had to wait several days for a reply; her letter arrived only this morning, with the trial due to begin tomorrow.

Dear Monsieur Aubert,

Thank you for your letter. I had to beg for paper and quill, but that is not the only reason it has taken me some time to respond. In truth, I was unsure how to respond. Your letter is very confusing, almost as if two entirely different people were writing to each other.

I have racked my mind as to what I might have done to harm you, but I am still unsure why you would be forgiving me. Perhaps you are merely offering my soul forgiveness in a pastorally manner before I face God's judgment. If that be the case, then I thank you. For I am not a perfect woman, and I am filled with regrets.

I would like to ask a favor of you. There is a young woman in Peissy who is heavy with child. Her name is Mireille Sanz. She will deliver soon, and, when I last examined her, the baby was yet to turn. I was due to turn it myself, but I was arrested before the day came. Would you be so good as to check on her for me? I am so anxious for her and for the child. It is very difficult to deliver a baby feet first, and there is no midwife nearby.

You wrote about our souls being intertwined, and I think there has been a misunderstanding between us. I laid my soul before you that day on the road to Geneva, and you did not lay down yours. Whatever feelings you have are yours alone. Not everyone has the same heart as you. And whatever feelings I might have been persuaded to have are gone.

I do not believe our souls are intertwined. If they were, I would not be in this prison today. But I do believe that you are a good man. I know you did not start this; I know you did not wish it to reach this point, and I believe you can still save your soul. Blessed is he that has it in his power to do evil, yet does it not. I also believe, remembering our conversations, that you are an admirer of St. Augustine, and so I would direct you to one of his sayings: "Right is right even if no one is doing it; wrong is wrong even if everyone is doing it."

You have more power than you know. I put myself in your trust.

Yours,

Louise

I read it again and again, a hundred times more. I spent most of the day reading it until it was dark outside. She is correct that there has been a misunderstanding between us, and there are so many clues that she does indeed have feelings for me. I laid down my soul...you are a good man...whatever feelings I may have had... It is understandable that she would be hesitant, cautious since she has to protect me from any association with an accused witch. And that in itself is evidence of her feelings. How to proceed, how to proceed?

✿ 18 ✿

ALEA IACTA EST

OCTOBER 24, 1545

The first day of the trial was finally upon us, and huge crowds had gathered outside the town hall. The whole city was in a frenzy of expectation, a frenzy that had helped its citizens through the wettest and coldest October in living memory. Louise de Peney, accused of witchcraft and with damning evidence against her, was not only a noblewoman but a Poor Clare. What better evidence of the evils of the Catholic church?

More anxious than usual, I had spent too long on the door-locking ritual as I left the house. With my mind occupied with thoughts of Louise, I was not fully concentrating on the procedure and required myself to go back and repeat it three times. By the time I arrived at the town hall, I had to push through the crowds outside, then squeeze past bodies in the aisles and on my row to take up my allotted position. By the time I sat, I was out of breath, and it helped somehow.

Louise was brought in backward, and when she was turned around, the first person she laid eyes on was me. I smiled at her, but she did not smile back. Perhaps to protect my anonymity. She looked at me with—I would have said pity, from her expression—but it could not have been. For who in her situation would pity someone like me, in my situation? It must have been sadness, for what else could it have been?

In just two weeks, she had lost much weight and looked so white and fragile. She was dirty too but had managed to tidy her hair under a bonnet. She answered all of Tissot's questions in a calm, strong voice, denying any suggestion of witchcraft. Tissot was unable to tie her in knots as he had done with some of the others.

"Did you give a potion to the wife of Jean Grippo when she was great with child that killed the child in the womb?"

"No. Sadly, the child was already dead in the womb when I arrived. There was no heartbeat. I gave Madame Grippo a tea of raspberry leaf and primrose oil to induce the fetus to come out."

"Let the court record that Mademoiselle Louise de Peney did indeed give a potion to a woman great with child."

"She would have died otherwise!" Louise protested, and there were gasps and jeers from the audience since a prisoner must not speak without being asked a question. "It was not a potion; it is a remedy that has always been used by midwives."

"And are you a licensed midwife, Mademoiselle?"

"Women are no longer permitted midwife licenses by the city of Geneva. There is no barber-surgeon in Choully or anywhere nearby. Tell me, what else should I have done?"

"Let the court note that Louise de Peney has been operating illegally as an unlicensed midwife."

It was a sparring match then, and there was near-silence in the court.

"You are remarkably calm and collected, Mademoiselle, for a woman in your position."

"If I am calm, it is only because my conscience is clear, my lord."

"May I propose to the court, at this juncture, that the lieutenant perform the crying test."

The lieutenant bade Louise come out of the dock and kneel before the panel of syndics. He placed a hand on her head and said, reading from a book, "I conjure you by the bitter tears shed on the Cross by our Savior the Lord Jesus Christ, for the salvation of the world, and by the burning tears poured in the evening hour over His wounds by the most glorious Virgin Mary, His mother, and by all the tears which have been shed here in this world by the Saints and Elect of God, from whose eyes He has now wiped away all tears, that if you be innocent, you do now shed tears, but if you be guilty that you shall by no means do so. In the name of the Father, and of the Son, and of the Holy Ghost. Amen."

Louise's eyes were closed, but her mouth was moving—she was lost in prayer.

"'Tis the sorcery of silence!" Tissot shouted.

"Nay, she cries!" someone called from the audience.

Her eyes were still closed, but tears streamed down her face, and her mouth quivered, then crumpled.

But Tissot had an answer for that. "'Tis only evidence that the Devil tricks us. As Cato says: 'When a woman weeps, she weaves snares. When a woman weeps, she labors to deceive a man.'"

In any case, Tissot was about to bring out the most damning evidence of all, which would turn her into the city's most hated witch.

"My esteemed syndics of Geneva, members of the audience, let it be known that a new item of evidence has come into our possession—a most grievous and damnable object." He paced the floor, building the tension. "As we all know, Satigny has been a venomous nest of plague-spreaders in recent months, but it appears that the most venomous of them all has so far gone free. Louise de Peney is an *engraisseuse,* a *bouteuse de peste*—a servant of the Devil!"

There was uproar; the city was still in the midst of the plague outbreak, and there was not a single citizen who had not lost a family member.

Louise looked at me with the beginnings of some understanding.

I felt myself reddening and looked at the floor.

Tissot waved a leather-bound volume—one of Louise's notebooks, the ones I had brought to him. "In this book, the accused writes, in great detail, of her plans to spread the plague to every Genevan citizen! The Devil's work, to be sure! Our investigators have found corresponding glass jars containing potions too dangerous to be brought here—too dangerous even to contemplate!"

Tissot went on to read extracts from Louise's diaries—her thoughts on planets, on women's bodies, on God—he held up her prized anatomical diagrams as if they were obscene pictures in the margins of some lewd poem.

By then, Louise was looking at me with horror and...with disappointment. She knew it was me. It was I who had sealed her fate. Why?

19

CONCUPISCIENTIAE

OCTOBER 25, 1545

"I would like to see Louise de Peney."

"State your business, please."

"State my business? Must a prison visitor have business?"

"Ordinarily, sir, no. But we've had several gentlemen coming down here to take their pleasure with her, you know. See what it's like with a witch. And a nun. Each one hoping they might be the first. No chance of that now, though—she ain't a nun no more. If you can manufacture a reason, I'll let you have a go. Not a bad time to, before she gets too filthy. Unless, of course, that's your thing."

"I am a city magistrate. I do not need to manufacture a reason. I need to question the prisoner."

"Alright, no harm intended. Follow me then."

So, she has been defiled... How do I feel about this? She is no longer a bride of Christ. Now, she belongs to all of us mortal men. She has lost that barrier of her dignity, and the gates have been opened. This gives me much food for thought. After the events of yesterday's trial, I decided to make the move and visit her. She probably has no more recourse to request visits, and our time may be short.

I had expected the city prison to have better conditions than that of Satigny, but how wrong I was. The smell was so powerful, it almost knocked me over. Human feces and human decay. I staggered and reached for the wall to steady myself, then wished I hadn't because my hand came away smeared in black slime and smelling foul.

The guard looked back at me as I fumbled to retrieve my pomander and put it to my nose. "Oh yes, you'll need that. It's bloody disgusting down here."

We passed several cells, and I tried not to look through the bars at what was inside. Louise was at the very end of the dark, damp corridor. While the guard fiddled with the huge set of iron keys jangling around his waist, trying to find the right one, I peered through the grille into the darkness, where I could vaguely make out a figure huddled in the corner. The door creaked open, the guard handed me his candle, and I stepped inside.

The figure was not moving, and I wondered for a moment if she was dead. There was enough light coming through the outside grille, along with my candle, for me to make out the floor space. She was wrapped in a blanket. It was freezing cold, and the walls were wet with damp.

I cleared my throat, and she still didn't move, so I said, "Hello, Louise."

Still nothing.

"Louise."

She stirred and squinted at me, keeping the blanket held up to her face. I moved closer with the candle so she could see me, but she still looked confused, as if she didn't recognize me.

"It is me, Henry. I have come to see you."

"Monsieur Aubert." It was neither a statement nor a question, and it hung in the air between us as if she was considering my purpose there or my very existence. It was disconcerting.

"How are you?"

She looked ever-so-slightly amused by the question. "I am as well as can be expected. Jacques kindly brought me food, clothes, and this blanket."

And now she calls him Jacques.

"I suppose it is not the first time you have been cloistered."

Her expression darkened. "I would hardly call this cloistered. And it is hardly the time for you to finally begin practicing light-hearted conversation."

I had never heard her use sarcasm before, and I was wounded. "I came to say... I came to give you some legal advice before the investigation and trial. Just tell the truth, Louise. I believe in justice."

"I believe in God's justice, certainly. But I wonder if God has a different purpose for me. I will try my best to tell the truth."

"You are strong."

She did not reply.

"I bring you good news."

She looked up expectantly.

"The baby in Peissy was born safely. I sent a messenger last night, and he returned this morning. A girl."

She nodded but looked a little deflated.

"I thought you would be pleased."

"I am pleased for her, of course. But, as you can imagine, I have other preoccupations at the moment."

"Can I bring you anything?"

"You could have brought me something today. But you did not."

"I...didn't know if you needed anything."

She opened her mouth to speak and then stopped and smiled to herself.

Why did I not bring something? Why do I never think? I immediately became distracted imagining all the books I could have brought her, all the conversations I could have started with a gift.

"Do not worry about me, sir. I have had plenty of visitors."

"You have?"

"Oh yes. I understand this is quite a notorious case. Jacques, of course, has been several times. Many men have come." She shuddered and looked away. "Marie Dentière came a few days hence. The last time I saw her, I was still a Clarisse. She came to set me free, then, into the bonds of marriage. How I disappointed her. And how I have had my comeuppance. She promised to plead my cause, but it will do no good. Will you plead my cause, sir?"

I managed to avoid answering directly. "You know how this goes. You will not be spared. One trial is like another. One torture after another will follow until you say that you are a witch. I wish I had spoken before."

"You can still speak for me."

"I cannot. It has gone too far now. I cannot turn back the wheels of justice. No, I mean that I wish I had spoken...about us...when I had the chance..." I hoped she would leap in and help me with that conversation, as people have so often done these past weeks when they have seen me struggle.

"Why are you here, Monsieur Aubert? Do you think I am really a witch? Perhaps I am. It is so confusing. I could not save that baby; I could have done more. For all those babies, all those mothers. I did not do enough, I was selfish, and now I will pay the ultimate price. I will renounce God so that He will not forgive me. I shall take my place in Hell, and I am ready, for I deserve it."

"No, no, if this is God's Divine Will, then nothing you have done can change His plan for you, Louise. You will take your place in Heaven, and one day, I will see you there."

She laughed, and there were traces of her old laughter. I say old, yet it was only a few weeks ago that we laughed together. How things have changed again. "You forget, magistrate, that I am not of the reformed faith." I must have looked shocked because she delighted in it and laughed more. "There, you see, I am a heretic, and therefore justice will be done because heretics must burn, must they not?"

"But you told me that—"

"I lied to you because I was afraid. They can take my body and my spirit, but they cannot take my soul. Where is your soul?"

I came away from our meeting dissatisfied, disconcerted. It is never enough, is it?

20

PANEM ET CIRCENSES

OCTOBER 26, 1545

Since Louise had not responded to merciful treatment, today, the process was adjourned to the Small Chamber. They removed her garments and shaved her, and she looked at me the whole time, her eyes only taken from mine when one of the barber-surgeons moved between us or bid her to turn this way or that. I felt it was a very powerful moment between us, and I was proud of my fortitude in controlling the temptations to pleasure that came to me. Now that her circumstances have been so reduced, now that I possess her fate, I feel more able to include her in my private fantasies.

During the witch-pricking, the investigators fell upon a scar on her hip. There was much discussion, much bobbing of raven heads, and every needle was used. I saw them gather around her hip, peering at it, then conversing, then peering at it again. She emitted no sound, so there was much scribbling of quills. They had found something. I knew what it was, and I knew that it was not the mark of the Devil. It was the ten-year-old scar from when Louise had fallen in the Arve during her escape from the Poor Clares. It was not the Devil's mark. Or perhaps it was, and she has been tricking me all this time, doubly, triply, deceiving me. That was certainly possible.

Since they discovered this mark, they had no need to examine her most intimate folds or use the pear-shaped implement. I imagined raising my hand to tell them that the mark on her hip was innocent, so they would be obliged to continue their investigations. But, of course, I did not and was disappointed. I shall have to use my imagination.

During her trials on the strappado, I consoled myself with thoughts of women who had chosen to endure horror and disgust in honor of our Lord. Catherine of Siena would suck the pus from cancerous breasts. Marguerite Mary Alacoque would eat the feces of dysentery-ridden men. They did it by choice, and it was all justified to bring about an ecstatic merging with the suffering body of Christ. This is no small comfort, and it elevates Louise to the ranks of martyrdom already.

In faith, it is as painful for me to be in love with Louise as it is for her to be tortured. I would do anything to have these feelings taken away. No, that is not true. I am a martyr to my feelings, like St. Catherine of Siena, feasting on the rotting foulness lying at the edges of things.

Louise held out in the strappado far longer than I have ever seen in a prisoner. She was raised, lowered, jolted, and wiggled; weights were added, taken away, and added again, but her strong arms held out.

Tissot roared at her, so loud and close that her ears must have been tortured as well, "Did you renounce God? Do you renounce God?" As if he was the Devil himself, demanding that she condemn herself to him.

I willed her to give in and also willed her to hold out, for it was the most exquisite torture for me, too.

But eventually, she could take no more and gasped, "I confess. Let me down."

The floor beneath her was a pool of blood, and she was rudely dropped into it in a heap, her drooping shoulders clearly broken. She scrabbled and slid in the mess to get to a kneeling position.

"When did the Devil first appear to you, Louise de Peney?"

"The Devil came to me just a few weeks hence. In the forest in Satigny."

"What form did he take?"

"He was tall and handsome, and he wore a long black cloak."

"What did he bid you do?"

"He tempted me in all manner of things, with charms and kindness and intellect."

"Did you copulate with him?"

"Many demons have copulated with me. All in the form of mortal men."

"How many times did the Devil visit you?"

"He visited me last night in prison. And he commanded me to deny everything."

Tissot opened his hands to the audience, to the syndics, as if that was the clinching piece of the puzzle. "Good people of Geneva, it is well known that the Devil oftentimes appears to the accused in prison to reinforce their allegiance! Now, there are six essential activities that a woman must commit in order to qualify as a sorceress. Namely: a pact with the Devil, sexual relations with the Devil, assembly at a Sabbath, magic, the slaughter of babies, and aerial flight. Madame de Peney has already confessed to five of these activities. So, I ask you now, Madame, have you engaged in aerial flight with the Devil?"

Louise, whose head had been hanging in exhaustion, chin almost touching her chest, looked up, and her eyes met mine with a mixture of recognition and bitterness. "Yes, I flew with the Devil. We rode together on the back of a long-tailed star."

She was thinking of me! The long-tailed star is our story! No matter that she conflated me with the Devil. If she is indeed a witch, then of course she would love the Devil, and if she is not a witch then...well, love and hate are so thinly separated. She still thinks of me.

❧ 21 ❧

MEA CULPA

OCTOBER 27, 1545

Sentencing will take place tomorrow, so this evening was my last chance. I entered the prison with a strange conviction that everything would be alright, that Louise would fix it, that some sort of Heaven-sent answer would present itself. Time rushes ahead, and I do not want this to be over.

She was naked, shaven, covered in bruises and scratches, and her own filth. One of her teeth had been knocked out. Her shoulders were dislocated so that her shape was deformed, and one ankle was broken so she could only crawl. Even in the darkness, I could see that her eyes were red as if the Devil had tried to wrench them from their sockets. She was a monster, and barely alive, at that.

She was motionless for so long that I thought she might be dead already until she spoke to herself or God—I didn't know for sure that she had even seen me. "So now you have my confessions, for which I must die. And they are sheer lies and made-up things. Or are they? Perhaps I was guilty. I should have saved more babies and more women —I did not study hard enough, I did not know enough. Perhaps I did cause those hailstorms when I went fishing and worried the water— perhaps I set off a wave that grew and grew and reached the heavens. All these things are possible. The village protected me for too long.

Perhaps I should have remained a Poor Clare. I suppose I renounced my vows, did I not? Poverty? I have been living in a palace. Obedience? I ran away from my deaconess and lived under my own rules. Chastity? Well, I tried. But that has now been taken from me many times over."

I sat in the crepuscule, still wondering whether she knew I was there.

"I must say that I am a witch, though I am not. I must renounce God, and then I will go to Hell. I would rather endure brief Hell in this world, then Heaven in the next. God wills it. And whatever God wishes, that is my wish too."

I suppose that, having confessed to a lie, she has, in effect, renounced God, and while that may be a trick by the court, it does mean that she has gone to the Devil. Because once they renounce God, they are real witches anyway. Can it be possible that I love a witch?

"You are very tiring to be with, Henry."

I suddenly realized she had been talking to me. Her voice was so faint, I could hardly hear.

"Have you heard of anchoresses, Aubert? Anchorites and anchoresses? There are many more anchoresses than the male equivalent. They would wall themselves in and were considered dead to the world. Devoted to a life of contemplation. You have managed to create your own anchoresses here. If they tried to escape, they would be burned. That is my fate, whether I try to escape or not. But you are more of an anchorite than I will ever be because you have walled yourself into your mind."

22

VOLUNTATEM DEI

OCTOBER 28, 1545

"We, the syndics, judges of criminal causes and of the city, having seen the process drawn up in form, and brought before us, at the instance of our lieutenant, against thee, Louise de Peney, of the *mandement* of Satigny and latterly of the Poor Clares, in said causes against thee, and by thy voluntary confessions made in our hands, and several times reiterated, it is to us manifest and evident that you, Louise de Peney, are guilty of the crimes of sorcery and heresy, things horrible, scandalous and infectious to all. Having exerted thyself to infect the world with your poison..."

The list of her crimes was so long that the moment of tension turned to tedium. It seemed there had been no misfortune or illness or death with which she had not been involved and to which she had not confessed her guilt.

"...For these causes and others, having consulted with our fellow citizens, and invoked the name of God to give a righteous judgment, sitting as a tribunal in the face of our elders, having God and His Holy Scriptures before our eyes. By this our definitive sentence, which we here render in writing, we condemn thee, Louise de Peney, to be bound and taken to the place de Champel, and there to be attached to a stake, and burned alive, until thy body be reduced to ashes; and thus, shall thy days be ended, to give an example to others, who might wish to commit like offense. And to you, our lieutenant, we commend our present sentence, commanding you to put the same into execution."

As the hammer fell upon the gavel, a roar rose from the crowd, cheers mingled with gasps of shock and cries of both approval and disapproval.

I studied Louise's face, so pale and emaciated that she was almost a skeleton already, for emotion. There was undoubtedly fear, along with the dignified acceptance that I had expected.

Engrossed in her face and jostled by crowds moving towards the exits, it took a moment for me to realize that someone was shouting at the jurists' bench and that someone was Bernard, who was standing next to me.

I shrank back and tried to keep my face neutral, lest anyone think to associate me with him.

Bernard shouted, "Would the lieutenant kindly confirm that she will be hanged first? She will be hanged first, will she not?" There was rising panic in his voice.

The syndics filed out, leaving Louise to the two jailers, and the lieutenant waved his hand vaguely towards Bernard as if to dismiss his point.

But Bernard did not give up and began pushing his way to the end of the row, shouting louder. "Sirs! In cases of witchcraft, it is customary to hang the prisoner before burning the body. Kindly confirm that this will be the case with Louise de Peney at Champel!"

A hush had fallen over the crowd, and people had stopped filing out, so the lieutenant sighed, and the robed figures stopped to hear his address. "Sir. Pastor Jacques Bernard of Peney, I believe? You are correct that, in most witchcraft cases, the bodies are hung first, but in cases of the most severe heresy, a more grievous punishment is required, and the body must be commended directly to Satan."

"I must protest—"

"You will sit down, sir, unless you wish to declare yourself a witch defender, in which case, the next trial may be yours. Do you wish to declare yourself a witch defender?"

There was silence in the courtroom as everyone waited to see whether the spectacle would continue.

But Bernard backed down, looking ashamedly at Louise.

23

DE CIVITATE DEI

NOVEMBER 1, 1545

The first day of November, All Saints' Day—a perfect day for a display of righteous judgment, although we are no longer permitted to celebrate saints' days since Calvin's edict of 1543, of course. The city was shrouded in fog. It rolled in from the lake like an army of slow ghosts. The white winter cloud having descended, the Jura, Alps, and Valais had disappeared. It was unlikely to lift until spring, other than the odd glimpse of a snowy peak.

Even in the city streets and squares, the mist swirled. It was the Sabbath, and instead of being their usual hive of activity, the city's labyrinthine streets and squares were deserted—the whole population already making their way to Champel and the Field of Execution. It would have been an excellent day for plague-spreading or house-breaking, I thought to myself, but I was not even momentarily tempted to stay at home, for I had to be there for Louise.

The only people left in the city were the little crowd standing outside the Bourg-du-Four, waiting for her to emerge. And emerge she did at nine o'clock, as La Clémence rang its warning to all devils —a Devil's servant herself emerged from the heavy wooden doorway onto the raised platform, accompanied by the lieutenant, a syndic, and two gaolers. Louise's hands were tied in front of her body, and the gaolers, one of whom held the end of the rope, each held one arm.

Surrounding the Bourg-du-Four gate were perhaps one hundred soldiers, their halberds jostling and clanging with no purpose other than ceremony. The lieutenant made his formal announcement of her execution, and then the sorry procession began towards Champel.

It is perhaps fitting that the prison entrance at Bourg-du-Four is almost directly opposite that of the *Hôpital Général*, the former home of the Poor Clares. So, almost exactly ten years ago, Louise had been rudely escorted from the city of her birth by soldiers.

And there she was again, being escorted even more rudely. The wind picked up again as if the air itself was bearing her out of the city. The Devil was on that wind. La Bise was coming. Last time, she had slipped away towards a new future, but there would be no chance of another escape.

I mulled it over for a while; imagine if she did escape. Imagine if there was some sort of commotion or distraction and, amongst the chaos, she slipped her guards and was lost in the crowd, would find my hand, and I would finally lead her to safety like I should have done ten years ago. We would cross the Jura before the snows grew too thick and make a new life together. But that was a fantasy for me to enjoy at a later stage. And, if I prefer stories to the truth, where is the harm? And, if I prefer to live with my stories than to live with people, where is the harm?

But I needed to concentrate on the moment because every detail would fill in my replaying of that day for years to come. I followed her, wanting and not wanting her to see me.

We approached Champel, and I had never seen such a large crowd, not even for the mass plague-spreading executions of that spring. Almost every one of Geneva's ten thousand inhabitants must have been there. The atmosphere was perhaps more somber, less carnivalesque than at the previous Satigny trials. There was real fear, for that day would see the destruction of a genuine servant of Satan.

I had to maneuver to find myself a viewing position, forgoing my pomander in order to use both hands to push. I had decided not to take my place with the other magistrates on their private platform because I was suddenly afraid of meeting her gaze. She would know I was there, and that would be sufficient. It was perhaps my little rebellion against the state machine. I was not a part of it anymore. But I was beginning to regret that decision, so jostled was I by the crowd that, despite my height, I was frequently almost lifted off the ground by the surges. I saw a party from Satigny, Donzel amongst them, and I wanted to see him laughing, celebrating, as he had done at the previous burnings. That would have provided some comfort to me, some assuaging of my guilt. If I could just see this as a common spectacle, a correct and normal outcome, simply the way of things. But Donzel looked subdued. I decided I wanted to be closer to her, so during one of the surges of bodies, I launched myself forward a few places toward the pyre. I regretted that decision as well, for I found myself next to none other than Bernard.

I nodded. "Good morning, Monsieur Bernard."

He looked at me with an expression I couldn't read, and he didn't respond. He appeared to be in a state of extreme agitation.

I leaned in to speak to him, raising my voice over the din of the crowd. There were some things I needed to know, and the finality of the situation emboldened me. "I need to ask you something."

"Must it be now?"

"It is about Louise. I saw you with her the night before her arrest. What were you doing there?"

I finally had his attention, and he turned to face me. He began with a raised voice but had to lower it to a whisper when he realized he was attracting attention. "I went to warn her, to beg her to leave. I knew they would be coming for her. I should have known it long before that. I asked for her hand—I would have gone with her; we could have gone to France that night, claiming asylum. But she refused."

"Why did she refuse?"

"She said that it would be a sin to make those vows when her heart was taken; she was already promised to another and that he would love and protect her."

"She said that?"

"Yes. She is married to God. She is a bride of Christ."

I nodded, but inwardly, my heart leaped because he believed she meant God, but I knew the truth. I was the one who took her heart! Yes, she had conflated me with the Devil back in the courtroom, but with Bernard, she had conflated me with God! What a presence I have had in her thoughts! As I have asked myself many times: if I think of someone constantly, does it mean I am in love? The answer is yes, and she did love me! Why did I not act sooner? What a fool I had been.

But the pastor was still talking, although he was looking around nervously because a hush had fallen over the crowd since the bells were chiming eleven.

"So, I told her to go to Annecy, where she should have gone nine years ago. They would forgive her, take her in, and she would only have to do penance. But again, she refused. Said she would never be cloistered again. She believed you would protect her, Aubert. She thought you were a good man. And now she is a martyr. Do you think you are a good man?"

What a question. I have always thought of myself as good, but perhaps we all think of ourselves as good. Even the Devil believes he is right. Eventually, I offered: "I obeyed my instructions at all times and followed the scriptures and the law."

Bernard appeared to ignore me. "I can only pray it will be quick. I am here to share a little of her suffering."

"Yes, me too."

"Stand aside, stand aside." The cart jostled the crowd as it moved through. A stake had been fixed into the ground, surrounded by firewood, straw, and kindling. There was a protracted discussion between the gaolers and the executioner about how she should be affixed to the stake. It was almost farcical and attracted jeers from the crowd.

But, in truth, I was grateful because it prolonged our final moments together in this world.

Finally, she was affixed with an iron chain around her body and several turns of rope around her neck. A crown of straw was placed on her bald head and sprinkled with sulfur in order to speed the burning.

The lieutenant, standing on the platform next to the pyre, shouted, "Behold! That woman whom they are about to burn... Behold her in the hands of the Devil, who will not release her grasp. Keep good watch over yourselves, for fear Satan should do the same to you. Hearken, Satan is about to seize upon her soul."

He had to raise his voice even louder because the wind picked up. La Bise had truly arrived, and the plateau of Champel is the most exposed part of the city. Bonnets were fastened tightly around chins, hats blew away, dogs barked, a flock of geese departing for the winter battled to hold their V-shape and eventually gave in and landed on the choppy Arve.

I realized Bernard was speaking to me.

"It has been known for people to dramatically withdraw their charges at the scaffold. I have seen it done."

"But those who accused Louise are now dead. It is not possible."

"There is one accuser who still lives." He had been looking straight ahead at Louise, but he turned his gaze to me. "You."

"I did not—"

"You are the only accuser who still lives. You are the one who brought the physical evidence to the case. The rest was rumor and gossip."

I said nothing, and he turned his whole body towards me.

"There is no in-between with you, is there? You have gone from poor orphan directly to city councilman, from shy recluse to celebrated witch-hunter, from chaste bachelor to jilted lover, all in a few weeks. You have hidden inside this city your whole life. Why not make this the moment when you reveal your true self? When you reveal that you are good?"

He had taken me by the shoulders and turned me towards him, but I could not meet his eye, looking at the cathedral spires behind him. Eventually, he wilted. "But you will not. You are too ashamed to speak for her. As was I."

I believe I did consider it at that moment. I no longer needed to punish her since it appeared she did not, after all, betray me with Bernard. But at this late stage, with her a convicted witch, I would be placing myself in grave danger as a witch defender. The crowd was ready for a spectacle, and in all likelihood, we would both be burned. There was, of course, the possibility that she was a witch; the evidence against her was indeed overwhelming, and if that was the case, then her execution was just. And if she was not a witch? I had already reconciled myself to the possibility of her martyrdom. It would be a beautiful thing, in truth, and she would wait for me to join her in Heaven while I live out my life working towards Calvin's godly society. No, it was too late to act.

We turned back to the pyre, and the executioner held a flaming torch aloft. Cheers erupted from the crowd as he placed it in the pile of wood. It gradually burst into flames.

Louise's face contorted into shapes I had not seen, the whites of her eyes so large, her mouth twisting into different grimaces, her lips moving in prayer all the while. Clouds of sulfurous smoke gradually obscured her, and she was quiet until the moment the flames rolled up to devour her face when she uttered a howl so terrifying that the crowd became quiet.

For a moment, my gaze fell on the gap where Donzel had been standing, and I saw that he had doubled over to vomit.

With the crowd hushed, Bernard spoke again, and I wished he wouldn't. His voice kept cracking, perhaps due to the smoke. "Have you ever thought about what Hell is like, Aubert? Have you been to Berne, to the cathedral, and seen the Last Judgment sculpted above the main portal? Have you ever seen a painting of Bosch?"

I had done none of those things because I had never traveled further than Satigny.

"Have you read Dante's Inferno?" he asked, although he was talking more to himself.

"Ah, yes. Well, of course, I imagine it is like that."

But he was not listening. "Grotesquely specific tortures, fiery punishments, indeed. Well, here we are. There you have the demons with pitchforks," he said, pointing to the two gaolers stoking the flames with long sticks. "And, all around us, the masses of lost souls, condemned to live with the symptoms of disease." With perfect timing, the man behind us erupted into a hacking cough, and when we looked, we saw his face beset by weeping red pustules. I instinctively reached for my pomander.

Louise went quiet, her body black and melting, but her eyes were still open, and her chest still moved with faint breaths.

I so desperately wanted Bernard to stop talking.

"Remind me, Aubert, what lies at the very pit of Dante's Hell? What is the Ninth Circle?"

I swallowed. "A frozen lake."

"And who is trapped in the ice?"

I knew the answer, but I did not speak because of the lump in my throat. Because I knew those people trapped in Dante's ice are perhaps not altogether dissimilar to myself.

"Betrayers, Aubert. Traitors, oath-breakers, and betrayers. Those who deny God's love through their denial of human ties, of human warmth. This is set to be a cold winter. I imagine our great lake will freeze come December. I will see you there, Aubert. I will see you there." He turned and left.

Good God, what did I set in motion? I pushed this thought to the back of my mind repeatedly. No, it was not I who set it in motion, and I could no more have started it than I had any power to stop it. It was God's justice. It was God's justice. Whatever the truth here on Earth, God has a plan for Louise.

After all the uncertainty in my mind, everything became clear. This was God's plan all along. I had no free will in it, but I am honored to be a part of it. Of this martyrdom. I resolved not to move from my position until her body was nothing but ashes. I would be with her until the end.

❧

When criminals are hung at Champel, or indeed at any of the other gallows around the city—on the bridge or in the marketplace—the bodies are usually left to rot. These swinging corpses serve as an effective warning to would-be criminals. In winter, they sometimes dangle there for months, frozen solid or covered in snow. In summer, they begin to decay and stink within days, fed upon by rooks and rats until only the bones are left, and they fall to the floor. No criminal can be buried in the consecrated ground of the cemetery, so the skeletons are simply left here, in that field of the dead. With Champel one giant charnel tomb and the plague cemetery on the other side of the city walls filled with thousands of bodies, the whole of Geneva is a veri-table boneyard. It will one day collapse under the weight of those bones.

But, with witches, it is different. Their bodies must be completely annihilated from existence to destroy any remnants of Satan. The cinders of a witch must be dispersed into flowing water to remove any trace of the body. But today, the wind was too strong for the gaolers as they battled to shovel Louise's ashes into sacks to be taken over to the bank of the Arve. La Bise whipped her up, each tiny fragment of her, and blew her to freedom, just like the first time she was hounded from the city. I like to think she has found her freedom again.

They say La Bise is a wind that only appears in Geneva. They say it makes people go temporarily mad—that it appears at the end of some period of tumult. They sometimes call it La Bise Satanée or La Bise Noire. The Kiss of The Devil. The Black Kiss. The air became speckled with Louise; flakes of her fell on people's clothing, making them sneeze and spit her from their lips. There were screams of "'Tis the Devil's poison, flee!"—some were screams of terror, others of hilarity. Children danced and chased and reached up to grasp the flakes in their hands, just as they do when the first snows arrive. Today, it snowed black.

24

POST TENEBRAS LUX

FEBRUARY 1, 1546

Post Tenebras Lux: "After the darkness, light." That is the new motto of our reformed city of Geneva, as decreed by Calvin and the city fathers. It already appears on our coins, our flags, and our armor, and is gradually being engraved all over the city. Before the Reformation, the phrase was *Post tenebras sperum lucem*: "After the darkness, I hope for light." From the Book of Job, of course. But Calvin has adapted it to reflect the new certainties of our faith. We can rejoice in the knowledge that everything that happens is the will of God.

I write this diary entry from my new home. I sit at my desk, which overlooks Louise's herb and vegetable beds, perfectly tended, yet coated with a blanket of snow. I shall do my best to keep them as she did. No doubt I can employ someone from the village to help me. We certainly had difficult beginnings, but I feel sure that I will be accepted and respected in Satigny. As the only notary, I shall make myself useful and, perhaps at the next city council elections, I will take over from Donzel as *châtelain*. After all, it is thanks to me that this village was finally extirpated of the witchcraft that had scourged it. And, when the council hears about their current *châtelain's* night-time antics and tax-collecting irregularities, I am sure they will demand he be replaced.

It is only right that I was offered Louise de Peney's worldly goods and chattels, which I happily accepted in lieu of payment for my services during the investigations and trials. On top of the sale of my parents' house in rue Tabazan, I am doing quite well for money now, and I will not miss that sad dwelling in the slightest.

I only arrived in Satigny yesterday with my furniture on a horse and cart. I attempted to enlist a couple of village boys to help me unload, but when I called out to them, they ran away. Perhaps they did not wish to work in such cold weather. This is indeed the coldest winter in the city's memory. The lake had completely frozen over when I left Geneva, children slipping and sliding, a lone abandoned fishing boat trapped far out until the spring thaw. Loosened from its moorings, it became trapped in the center of the frozen lake.

I went to the Peney Inn last night to dine and to attempt to procure a housekeeper—I think it is high time I had some help commensurate with my elevated station. I even thought of Pernette; it would certainly be a step up in the world for her, too. But strangely, nobody was talkative in the inn last night.

Madame Rolette served me in silence. I thought I may have heard her mutter something along the lines of, "Who does he think he is?" But I'm not sure of the meaning or if I even heard correctly.

Perhaps they need some time to grow accustomed to the fact that I am no longer their investigator but their friend and neighbor. How could they not be flattered that the magistrate who saved them from the Devil's scourges has chosen to live amongst them?

Because the truth is, I feel so intimately connected to this place now that I cannot imagine living anywhere else. I will revisit the places I went with Louise—the forest, the river, the prison. And replay our conversations and encounters to my heart's content.

Out the window, there is a flash of red against the white snow, and I see a squirrel dart across the garden, leaving tiny gossamer footprints. It stops briefly and looks up at the window before disappearing into the bushes. How strange to see a squirrel in the midst of winter when most wild mammals are asleep.

When I am settled, I will go through Louise's papers in fine detail. There is much excellent unfinished work here, to some of which she alluded. On astronomy, gardening and herbs, medicine. In particular, I would like to develop her studies on preventing the spread of plague. Had she lived, Louise would never have been able to publish her work under her own name. One only has to consider what happened to Marie Dentière. The moment she tried to publish under her own name, as a woman, her work was violently suppressed, destroying any chance for other women to make similar attempts. So, I am honoring Louise and Marie Dentière, as well as providing a valuable service if I claim the work as my own and show the world something that would never have seen the light of day otherwise. I am certain Louise would have wanted me to take the credit.

And, as Calvin continually reminds us, the new godly society must be built upon the foundations of the household, and women must take their places within the home, not waste their time writing. Otherwise, the foundations will collapse.

In any case, Louise will not know any of this. While I admire Calvin's industry, I refute his ideas in *Psychopannychia*. I have come to believe that he is wrong in his interpretation of soul sleep. Indeed, he may be wrong about many things. After all, we cannot always be right. Calvin says that death is but a separation of the body from the soul—that the soul does not sleep until the Day of Judgement but lives with the saints, enjoying Paradise. I cannot bear the idea of Louise living without me, enjoying heavenly delights I cannot imagine.

In any case, Calvin forgets that this idea is reminiscent of Purgatory, the Catholic heresy that we have now erased. No, in this case, I prefer Martin Luther's argument. Luther tells us that "as soon as thine eyes have closed shalt thou be woken, a thousand years shall be as if thou hadst slept but a little half hour. Just as at night we hear the clock strike and know not how long we have slept, so too, and how much more, are in death a thousand years soon passed. Before a man should turn round, he is already a fair angel." What beautiful words! And since Louise has no concept of the passing of time right now, she can have no complaint as to me staying on this Earth, living in her house, for the life she wanted to live cannot be lived by a woman. She will wait for me in blissfully deep soul sleep, and we shall enter Heaven together.

If she died a martyr, that is good. If she was indeed a witch, then her death is also justified, and she deserves to be in Hell without me. And so, I have nothing with which to reproach myself. There must be a time, in this life or the next, when we all come to know what we truly are. I know I am an instrument of God's Divine Justice and an architect of His Kingdom on Earth.

AFTERWORD
HISTORICAL NOTES

The Europe-wide "witch-craze" began in the fourteenth century and reached its peak in the years 1580-1630. Both Protestant and Catholic authorities encouraged it. An estimated 50,000 people were burned at the stake, 80% of them women. The *Malleus Maleficarum* (Hammer of Witches) was the most influential amongst a multitude of inflammatory, misogynistic texts that sanctioned the torture and execution of suspected witches.

Geneva played an active part in the witch craze. In the first three months of 1515, for example, 500 suspected witches were burned. As the century progressed, conviction rates dropped; however, the last witch to be burned in Geneva was Michelle Chauderon in 1652. The last witch to be executed in Switzerland was Anna Goldi in 1782. She was finally exonerated in 2007 when the Swiss Parliament acknowledged her execution as a miscarriage of justice.

In the 1520s, the city of Geneva began asserting its independence from the House of Savoy, forging alliances with other Swiss cantons and fighting a series of battles against the Duke of Savoy's armies. During this time, there was an influx of Protestant refugees into Geneva, and a number of influential preachers of the reformed faith established themselves in the city. In 1536, Geneva finally defeated Savoy, and the Grand Council turned the city into a fortress, destroying all the suburbs and surrounding castles, and bringing almost the whole population within new city walls. Only a few outlying rural *mandements* (administrative districts) remained, including Satigny (which comprised the scattered villages of Satigny, Peney, Peissy, Choully, and Bourdigny).

Geneva declared itself Protestant in 1536 and became regarded as the "Protestant Rome."

John Calvin, a French refugee, was based in Geneva from 1536 until his death in 1564 and wielded enormous power as the city's spiritual leader. He preached and wrote tirelessly and involved himself in the details of every aspect of city government and the lives of Geneva's residents. He established a welfare state and an education system, and is still regarded as the symbol and figurehead of Geneva. However, his reputation has a controversial side, in large part due to the death of his former friend, Michael Servetus, who he authorized to be burned alive in 1553 over a theological dispute.

This story is based on real historical events. Geneva suffered multiple plague epidemics, and there were several plague-spreading conspiracies in the mid-sixteenth century. In the spring of 1545, 45 people from the *mandement* of Satigny were executed for plague-spreading. In the autumn of that year, there were several accusations of witchcraft in Satigny, and it was the *châtelain* Donzel who brought them to the attention of the Small Council in Geneva. Calvin intervened in the case, demanding that "this race of witches be extirpated," and city investigators were sent to assist. Jacques Bernard was the pastor of Satigny at the time and was indeed the only former Catholic priest to be made a Reformed minister.

Antoine Froment was a leading Reformation preacher who taught the children of Geneva to read and write, free of charge, in the Place Molard. His wife, Marie Dentière, was a former nun who became an important Protestant activist and is the only woman to be commemorated on the Reformation Wall in Geneva. The Poor Clares were hounded from the city in 1535 and sought refuge at the monastery of

Annecy. Only two of them became Protestant and accepted husbands. Louise de Peney is a fictional character, as is Henry Aubert.

Halley's Comet was sighted over Europe multiple times in 1531.

APPENDIX A
LATIN CHAPTER TITLES

Crimen exceptum: a crime apart
In 1468, Pope Paul II issued a decree which declared that witchcraft was a *crimen exceptum*—a crime so extreme that normal judicial procedures need not apply, and torture could be used to extract confession.

Index Librorum Prohibitum: list of prohibited books
The Catholic church maintained an Index of Prohibited Books from 1560 until 1966. Calvin's regime in Geneva had its own list of banned books, including 'immoral' and Catholic works.

Sine diabolo, nullus dominus: without the Devil there is no God
A Latin saying that refers to the concept of dualism, which assumes there are two separate entities—good and evil—which are equally powerful.

Manum misi in ignem: I put my hand in the fire
Attributed to St. Jerome.

Secreta mulierum: secrets of women

Secreta mulierum was a late-thirteenth-century medical textbook, attributed to Albertus Magnus.

Sermones vulgares: vulgar discourses

Sermones Vulgares was a text by French theologian Jacques de Vitry (c.1160/70 - 1240).

Turpitudinem: disgrace/immorality

In legal terms, Nemo auditur propriam turpitudinem allegans ("Nobody is to be heard recounting his own turpitude") refers to the principle that indirect proof of guilt usually suffices for a conviction because of the rarity of confession.

Incurvatus in se: turned/curved inward on oneself

Incurvatus in se describes a life lived for oneself rather than for God and others. The phrase may have been coined by St. Augustine, and the condition was also described by Paul the Apostle: "I do not understand my own actions. For I do not do what I want, but I do the very thing I hate... For I know that nothing good dwells within me, that is, in my flesh. I have the desire to do what is good, but I cannot carry it out. For I do not do the good I want, but the evil I do not want is what I do. ." (Romans 7:15-19)

Alterius non sit qui suus esse potest: let no man be another's who can be his own

The motto of Paracelsus.

Psychopannia

The earliest theological treatise by Calvin, 1534. He opposed the 'mortalism' or 'soul sleep' taught by Anabaptists and other radical Protestants.

Odi et amo: I hate and I love

A short poem by Roman lyric poet Catallus, often referred to as Catallus 85.

Speculum stultorum: Mirror of fools

A popular 12th century satire, mentioned in the Canterbury Tales.

Caput galeatum: caul (literally 'helmeted head')

A baby born 'in the caul' is born with a piece of membrane covering the head and face, or is born inside the amniotic sac. It is rare but harmless and, in some traditions, was considered good luck.

Sola scriptura: by scripture alone

A Christian theological doctrine held by many Protestant and Reformed churches that considers the Bible to be the sole and infallible source of authority.

De praestigiis daemonum: on the tricks of demons

De praestigiis daemonum was a 1563 book by Johann Weyer, who claimed that witchcraft does not exist and that those who claim to practice it are suffering from delusions. It was influential in the abolishment of witchcraft trials in the Netherlands.

Si fallor, sum: I err therefore I am

Attributed to St. Augustine.

Osculum Infame: shameful kiss

The supposed ritual greeting of a witch upon meeting with the Devil, involving kissing the Devil's anus.

Alea iacta est: the die is cast

Attributed to Julius Caesar as he led his army across the Rubicon in 49 BC.

Concupiscientiae: lust

In Christianity, the tendency of humans toward sin. In his Confessions, St Augustine referred to concupiscence as sinful lust.

Panem et circenses: bread and circuses

A phrase attributed to the Roman satirical poet Juvenal to refer to a superficial act to appease the crowd.

Mea culpa: through my fault
From the Catholic confession.

Voluntatem Dei: God's will

De Civitate Dei: About the City of God
A theological work by St Augustine.

Post Tenebras Lux: Light After Darkness
The adopted motto of Calvinism and of the city of Geneva.

APPENDIX B
TRIGGER INDEX

- **Child death**
- **Death** (by hanging and burning)
- **Extreme misogyny**
- **Elder abuse** (torture)
- **Gore** (torture)
- **Torture** (medieval)
- **Sadism** (sexual)
- **Sexual assault** (implied)

ABOUT THE AUTHOR

Catherine Fearns is a writer and musician from Liverpool, UK. The first book in her bestselling *Reprobation* series won a Readers' Favorite Silver Medal and a Page Turner eBook Award. She has also been widely published as a music journalist, specializing in heavy metal. She plays guitar and keyboards in the all-female metal band Chaos Rising, and her sheet music compositions are published by Universal Edition. Catherine currently lives in Switzerland, and has four children, a Tibetan terrier and an axolotl.

Other Books by Catherine Fearns
The Reprobation Series:
Reprobation
Consuming Fire
Sound
Lamb of God
Buried Lightning (forthcoming)

THANK YOU FOR READING

Thank you for reading *All the Parts of the Soul.* We deeply appreciate our readers, and are grateful for everyone who takes the time to leave us a review. If you're interested, please visit our website to find review links. Your reviews help small presses and indie authors thrive, and we appreciate your support.

Other Titles by Quill & Crow

The Ancient Ones Trilogy

The Famine Witch

The Blood Bound Series

The Quiet Stillness of Empty Houses